THE MINDFUL PRESIDENT

*An Educational
Fictional Autobiography*

THE MINDFUL PRESIDENT

*An Educational
Fictional Autobiography*

GLENN BOYD SMITH

A version of this book was also self-published under the title, *The Empty Piñata President*.

© 2021 by Glenn Boyd Smith
All Rights Reserved
No part of this book may be reproduced in any form or by any electronic or mechanical means including information storage and retrieval systems without permission in writing from the publisher, except by a reviewer who may quote brief passages in a review.

Sunstone books may be purchased for educational, business, or sales promotional use. For information please write: Special Markets Department, Sunstone Press, P.O. Box 2321, Santa Fe, New Mexico 87504-2321.

Book and cover design › R. Ahl
Printed on acid-free paper
∞
eBook 978-1-61139-617-1

Library of Congress Cataloging-in-Publication Data

Names: Smith, Glenn Boyd, 1940- author.
Title: The mindful president : an educational fictional autobiography / by Glenn Boyd Smith.
Description: Santa Fe, New Mexico : Sunstone Press, [2021] | Summary: "With the help of others of good will, a modern leader's mindful insights into life's priorities and challenges enables him to skillfully and courageously lead action aimed at change in quality of life for himself and others"-- Provided by publisher.
Identifiers: LCCN 2020047635 | ISBN 9781632933164 (paperback) | ISBN 9781611396171 (epub)
Subjects: LCSH: Presidents--Mexico--Fiction. | Leadership--Fiction. | LCGFT: Fictional autobiographies.
Classification: LCC PS3619.M5863 M56 2021 | DDC 813/.6--dc23
LC record available at https://lccn.loc.gov/2020047635

WWW.SUNSTONEPRESS.COM
SUNSTONE PRESS / POST OFFICE BOX 2321 / SANTA FE, NM 87504-2321 /USA
(505) 988-4418 / FAX (505) 988-1025

DEDICATION

We live in a world that is facing many problems that are reaching a crisis state—a state where only extraordinary efforts and interventions might perhaps turn things around and prevent our extinction. The many factors involved in the problems of society are extremely complex, but at the base of possible solutions to these complex issues is individual personal behavior.

This work is dedicated to all who help others find happiness—to find freedom, justice, and equality, as well as freedom from hunger, disease, discrimination, crime and lawlessness, insecurity, tyranny, and the blatant abuse of power.

In particular, I dedicate this work to all leaders of society who hold to the principle that leadership is central to the foundation of human inspiration and social development. They clearly see that they are responsible to not only control and protect, but to educate, inspire, support, and appropriately use expert knowledge in the education and governance of the people they have chosen to serve. In this era, in acting upon what we know of the interrelatedness and interdependence of human life, this service extends to all peoples of the earth.

I dedicate this also to all who live without freedom, in poverty and suffering, many of whom are being brutally forced from their homes by corrupt and inept tyrants. They are victimized not only by their tyrannical leaders, but also by the lack of intervention by decision makers; by what is commonly seen as respecting the principle of self-determination. However, failure to intervene is really a denial of human rights and the negation of the self-determination of the victims, as they are kept from the precious rights to freedom, justice, and equality, within their own homes.

CONTENTS

9 | Preface

12 | Prologue: The Path, How to live

17 | Characters

19 | The Piñata: The definitive Mexican metaphor

21 | 1. Miguel: Who and What am I?

29 | 2. Strength in Weakness: Responding to Life's Challenge

37 | 3. The Secret Meeting: The Difficult Context of Change

45 | 4. Refuge: Retreat, Solitude, and Insight

48 | 5. Father Antonio: A Witness to Love

53 | 6. Bud and Stella: Thriving in Adversity

60 | 7. Héctor and Isabel: The Great Gift of Authentic Teachers

75 | 8. Massacre and Outrage: Pain and Suffering

89 | 9. The Plan: Enabling Structure

104 | 10. My Speech to the Nation: The Practical Application of Hope

117 | 11. The Empty Piñata: Hope amidst Ridicule

123 | 12. Reflections: Strength in Planning With Those Who Love

128 | 13. The Presentations: Supportive Witness to Our Needs

136 | 14. Diego: Great Anguish in Sacrifice

141 | 15. The Verge of Sadness: Carrying On

151 | 16. María: Continuing the Effort With hope and Love

162 | Epilogue: Elusive Hope of Ultimate Right Consequence

165 | Reading Guide

PREFACE

When I was young—in my questioning and rebellious youth, I lived with what I am now told is a common delusion. Although I never quite clearly articulated what I now see as a misconception, I thought that there was only one of the many clearly identifiable belief systems that was right and true, and if I could only find out which one, I would have attained a chief goal in life—how to live.

My search for my seemingly elusive goal has continued but is no longer a search for the absolute nor is it within the confines of 'one' nor in isolation from life's very complex but very individualistic experiences. This search, whether or not we are mindful of it, is, for all of us, at the basis of our lives. It is at the basis of this novel. Our challenge to be truly attentive, to learn, to act, to live in harmony with what is revealed to us in life, is articulated in this book. It centers on the personal and professional life of a fictional president. President Miguel, whom I hope becomes, at the same time, a friend and a companion in our search, as well as a model and one of our teachers.

Others' life stories often provide us, not only interesting and intriguing stories and information; they often give us knowledge and wisdom and add to the vicarious store of experience, which is so much a part of the value and gifts that come in our relationships. In addition to wanting to tell a fascinating and very interesting life-story, I hope to give to others a means of considering some of the important things that I have discovered in my experience and life-search, particularly in my relationships with others. The protagonist in this story finds knowledge and wisdom in this way.

We are often alone in thinking that we 'have the answers' to many of life's questions. However, we keep telling others of these "truths," not so much as to dictate what is right, but to explore and ask others to consider the validity of what we are saying. This is my intention in this work. I want others to consider what I see as essential issues, some critical, as well as consider practical application of a plan, if only in advocacy to implement solutions. The issues are not always explicitly stated in my writing. Many come only to the fore implicitly, in the behavior of the characters in this work. Many may even remain 'hidden' for some readers who enjoy and are entertained only by the very interesting life of President Miguel.

The sheer enjoyment of reading this work, along with any new insights into life's priorities, will, I hope, bring about a review of the practical application of our spiritual wellness. This aspect and the action springing from our value-system, is at the base of all aspects of wellness. Our physical, financial, psychological, emotional, intellectual, social, ecological, career, occupational, environmental and aesthetic wellnesses all depend upon our skillful behavior in application of our values as a foundation. I audaciously imply and intend that this book might well change some of the dysfunctional, corrupt, and destructive individual and collective behavior in our societies—changing the way we do things and bringing us from near destruction. I want to daringly encourage the evaluation of behavior, our needs, and the development and establishment of individual and collective plans to promote well-being, happiness and harmony in one's self and in the world.

I wrote this book for a wide audience. To accomplish this I intended it to be, at once—at the same time, entertaining, fascinating, enjoyable, educative, and prophetic and present a challenge to any reader. However, at the centre of this intent—my particular audience, are the leaders in our society, particularly educators and political leaders. It is my contention that the consistent failure to meet modern needs by governance is not in the fault of the systems—in the organizational structures that we have developed over many centuries, but in the individual behavior of our leaders. Corrupt, partisan, selfish behavior, which we so readily accommodate in our failure to advocate; is literally bringing the world to ruin.

One of the important core reasons for writing *The Mindful President* was to present what has been for me an important factor in all of my life's work. As a professional problem-solver, I learned early on that 'awareness alone is not enabling'.

In our so called 'developed societies' we have a tendency to treat the information in concepts as if it were a kind of 'end result'—often as a kind of mindless entertainment. Concepts and ideas about life are static. They are unchanging. My intent in this writing is to bring greater awareness to the need to look beyond, or perhaps below concepts and information, to direct experience and to individual behavior, to be actively and constructively mindful in our skillful attempts to improve the quality of life.

All life experiences, and particularly in relationships, can bring inspiration and abundant resources to talk and write about the human condition. My particular experience as an educator, particularly as professor of psychology and wellness and as a psychotherapist, have brought me, in addition to rich experience and resources, inspiration to write this novel. The shared experience of students and clients has helped me to look beyond psychological and mental-health concepts, to look to direct experience and to help identify and express some of the ideas and the explicit and the implicit recommendations that I make in *The Mindful President*.

I am grateful for my experiences with others—all who have provided a rich resource for everything that I do in life and in this particular instance the writing of this novel. I am grateful for my time and travels in Latin America. The direct experience of the concepts of the rich Mexican culture provided me with knowledge to describe the complex social environment in which the story of Miguel takes place.

An interesting phenomenon often occurs when we note, cite, learn of, or somehow deal with very significant issues. Often, shortly after we begin to 'see' these significant issues 'everywhere'. I write this preface during the pandemic of the year 2020. I see 'everywhere' the focus of attention and discussion of the causes and solutions to social problems turning to some of what our teachers have been telling us for millennium and to what I have attempted to reiterate. I feel a sense of accomplishment in that the poverty of my words might support mindfully bringing our attention to the base problems of the world as we more directly experience their symptoms.

It is my hope that the reader will thoroughly enjoy reading about President Miguel and his relationship with himself and others. I hope also that the reader will be reminded that his/her relationships and ours, are what we so much want to protect through paying close attention to our lives—by living mindfully and enacting upon the acquired insights.

PROLOGUE

The Path, How to Live

What is the meaning of life? To be happy and useful.

—Tenzin Gyatso, the fourteenth Dalai Lama

The path to happiness and relief from our suffering, or at least starting in a process to attain this, has always been one of the greatest challenges for human beings. In the profound confusion and suffering, that is part of the basic human condition, we are often overwhelmed by the immensity of it. We grasp at things that give only a temporary and fleeting sense of permanence, stability, or happiness. This path, while clearly evident in individual behavior, is often paralleled in collective behavior.

In our search for meaning, we are too often misled. We often put too much emphasis on one aspect of our search—on the *why* of life. We give validity to religions, philosophies, or subjective and individually assigned beliefs that only serve to give temporary refuge from the disagreeable things of life. This sometimes acts as a kind of entertainment, and we hide in the activity of it, the liturgical and cultural aspects of our involvement in these things. We sometimes escape, alone or with others, to live in a small, unreal, and seemingly protected world, and we become heedless of the greater reality of life and of our interdependency upon one another. We fail to see that these things are directly related to our happiness and peace of mind.

Some deny the reality of our fundamental condition of ignorance and our need to find a way, alone, and yet with others. Some act as though they are the centre of the universe and live accordingly, often within a closed system of dogmatic conviction and the belief that they have a monopoly on the truth. Many others lose their way through over-spiritualization, looking for magical solutions and saviours. They lose not only logic, but also freedom, and they incarcerate themselves in a fundamentalist prison that denies a reality beyond the chains that hold them in bondage, sometimes worshiping saviours or magic and forgetting the messages of their authentic teachers. They not only build but also live in proverbial castles in the sky.

We often fail to realize that the reason for existence—the great challenge to understand the *why* of existence—is almost irrelevant unless we find a way *how* to live. Only with this will we begin to actualize this great challenge and find great meaning in our lives as well as enjoy a sense of peace, happiness, and deliverance from the disagreeable things of life. This is true for all people, whether or not they see harmony and order in the universe, with or without gods, or with or without a clear reason for existence. We need to, as the Taoists have articulated it, "adjust to life" and find a way to live in some kind of balance and harmony and thus begin to enjoy the happiness we seek, which is, in fact, readily available to us.

At the heart of this great struggle, which extends to all humanity, is the individual, alone and yet together with others, struggling to find happiness and peace. This story is about an individual who lives in this age of war, conflict, hatred, and violence and who is caught up in this paradox of opportunity and crisis. It is about his response to the challenge of a search for this *how* of life. His search, like ours, is often muddled and confused and, like ours, brings sporadic and sometimes conflicting thoughts—thoughts that seem to be more in battle rather than in a process of coming to greater but still tentative truths. These are the truths that we are reluctant to risk in application, because of the fear and caution that exist so strongly in our various predispositions.

The setting for this story, apart from being in the mind of an individual, is Mexico, a beautiful country where the extremes of the effects of accumulated development and mis-development and the conflict that these bring are both important considerations in every aspect of daily life. Mexicans and Mexico are, in a sense, in a profound conflict with themselves and with one another for many reasons, including their historical development and because of the current problems of corrupt behavior and violence. It is the kind of violence that often comes from a root cause, which originates primarily beyond the borders of Mexico, but only in the sense that it is part of the common human experience. The failure to find a way to adjust to life amidst the violence and corruption, which is linked to drug dealing and drug use, is held fast by the power of addiction.

The meaning of life and the how of life are topics that can more easily be ignored or forgotten in other, more peaceful places, but not for long. The world of individuals is in crisis as thus are our collectives. This is a story that faces all human beings wherever we are and whatever conditions we live with or within. The individual struggle with the how of life often parallels a struggle in one's personal life and one's life in the worlds of work, family, vocation, or profession. This is the case in this story. The power of the influence and clash of the roles one plays in each of these worlds is also part of this story.

~~~

In light of the current knowledge and the opportunities that human development have brought, we might say that never before have we—and more so for those of us who do not live under tyranny—had such a unique opportunity to develop and enhance our search for a way to be that brings the promise of happiness and peace.

There are many things in our era that influence our individual search for quality of life and happiness. However, this is also true of the aspects of human life that have been collectively developed, as well as those things that have collectively been mis-developed and that we often follow. These lead us away from authentic happiness and peace. Although each individual's makeup and circumstance differs in each era, our era, which is arguably no more challenging and confusing than any other time, brings with it the threat of collective destruction and annihilation. This is the significant aspect of the time in which we live. The path to the acquisition of knowledge, which can create volition and action, perhaps was easier and clearer in former times. This is no longer the case in the modern world. The confusion brought about by the clashing new voices telling us how to live brings an element of fear to our individual search, and it is harder to listen and act upon the truth of our inner voices.

Individual development and mis-development end at death. Collective development and mis-development continue and grow to include additional aspects that are part of each era. This is particularly evident in the current increased global existence of fear, violence, and destruction and their growth in multiple proportions. The accumulated fear, fed by the many and very powerful means we now have to destroy one another, tends to lead to a kind of despair and isolation, a despair that is not immediately evident and that manifests itself in a false life. It is oftentimes manifested in violence and corrupt behavior. It also fosters a failure to see that there is a way to live and to trust in the hope of a productive interdependence that we can have with one another.

Every individual is, in some aspects of life, alone and at the same time together in this great challenge and search. Part of our task is to discover how to behave within this dichotomy in a responsible manner without misusing the anger that often comes in this situation, which prevents action that leads to unity and happiness. Individually we search; then we make decisions to practice "how" to live. Collectively, we bring this awareness and knowledge as a component in our behavior with others. In various ways we influence and are influenced in our behavior by our families, our social and work groups, our governments, our worldwide affiliations and associations, and our philosophies and belief systems. The leaders of society hold a unique role in the development and in the playing out of the challenge to find a better way to live. However, modern leadership simply does not respond to the needs that we face in our dilemma of the near destruction of our societies. The influence that comes from selfish and partisan alliances that support the use of control as a means of leading, results in the failure to provide the means of responding to the rights and the dire needs of the governed.

Never before have we had such a powerful paradox in the crisis that exists in individual and collective development and in the search for happiness and peace. We have so much wisdom and so many opportunities available in our search for these things, but at the same time we find ourselves in a world plagued with self-destructive violence, greed, and corruption, paradoxically based in our fear, anger, and frustration.

The *why* of human life, for many, is elusive and for many, if seen alone, is a futile search. The *how* of life, however, is readily available to us and can bring, without extraordinary effort, solutions to many of our problems. In the poverty of words, this story attempts to explain this and examines this search. It may bring new insights into our priorities and help lead to the search for this *how* of things.

How to live, given the state of the world and the apparent overwhelming task this implies, might well reduce us to despair. We must, however, remember that we are not the saviours of the world. We are called to be grateful in seeing the harsh reality of problems and to work toward change, but we are not responsible for the totality of transformation. Remembering that we might well see our dual task—transforming ourselves and helping to transform the world and its organizational structures—as always being unfinished.

"The day is short and the task is great… You are not required to complete the work, but neither are you free to abstain from it."

—Ethics of the Fathers

CHARACTERS

Miguel—Juan Miguel Soto Rios, President of the United Mexican States

María—María Ángeles Santos Aguilar, Miguel's wife

Lalo (Eduardo), Miguel and María's son

Malena (María Elena), Lalo's wife

Maribel (María Isabel), Miguel and María's daughter

Nacho (Ignacio), Maribel's husband

Diego—Juan Diego Soto Ríos, Miguel's brother

Marta Ana, Diego's wife

Olivia, Diego and Marta Ana's granddaughter

José, Miguel's household butler

Don* Alfredo—Doctor Alfredo Alonso Rodríguez Alfaro, Senator and old friend and advisor of Miguel

Cristina, friend of María

Doña* Margarita—Ana Margarita Robles Martínez, Miguel's personal secretary

Don Alberto Rodríguez Robles, a retired Spanish Supreme Court judge

Alfonso Mario Xaxalpa y Xaxalpa, a respected indigenous leader and friend of Miguel

Cardinal Contreras, church official and friend of Miguel

Padre Toñio, Father Antonio—Father Jose María Antonio Ruiz Alfaro, old family friend and parish priest in Santa Clara de las Flores

Bud and Stella—Gordon Smart and Estella María García Durán, retired American-Mexican couple living in Mexico, friends of Miguel

Liz, Bud and Stella's daughter

David, Liz's husband

Monica, Liz and David's daughter

Lupita (Guadalupe), Bud and Stella's live-in maid

Agustina, Guadalupe's mother

Héctor and Isabel—Doctor Héctor Guzmán Ruiz and Doctor María Isabel Alfaro Fuentes, professors, friends of Miguel

Romero, one of Miguel's security personnel

Doctor Anselmo Gutierrez, Miguel's trusted cabinet member

Jorge Maldonado, a governmental official

David Lalonde, former prime minister of Canada and friend of Miguel's

Don Pedro Alfaro Ruiz, indigenous farmer

* The title Don (Don for a man, Doña for a woman) is an honorific title of European origin. It was originally reserved for royalty, nobles, and church officials. It is now often used as a mark of esteem for people of personal or social distinction.

THE PIÑATA

The Definitive Metaphor for Mexico

Dale, dale, dale, no perdas el tino,
Porque si lo perdes, pierdes el camino

Hit, hit, hit, don't lose your aim,
Because if you do, you lose your way

—The *Piñata Song,* traditionally sung while breaking the piñata.

The piñata is a brightly decorated clay pot or papier-mâché figure, filled with sweets, fruit, and toys. It is hung up at various celebrations and struck with a stick by blindfolded children who hope to break it or knock it to the ground in order to open it and release and enjoy the contents.

The piñata originated in China and was brought to Europe in the fourteenth century, where it was incorporated into Lenten celebrations. The Spaniards brought the custom to the Americas, although they found that the American indigenous peoples already had very similar customs. The Aztecs used a type of piñata in celebration of their war god. The Mayans used it to play a game in which the participants were blindfolded. The Spanish missionaries united the traditions to be used for Christian religious instruction during Lent, decorating clay pots with very bright and attractive colours that represented the enticement of temptation. The decorated pots represented Satan or evil. They were decorated with seven cones or horns, which represented the seven deadly sins of pride, greed, lust, envy, gluttony, wrath, and sloth. The sweets and fruit inside the piñata represented the temptations, related to earthly pleasures and wealth, and the stick represented virtue in combat with temptation. The blindfolded participant represented "blind" faith defying evil as well as the hope that good efforts bring. In addition to faith and hope, the beautiful decorated piñata represented charity in the form of blessings and gifts from a merciful God.

Although today much of the religious or spiritual symbolism is no longer a part of the celebrations of breaking the piñata, it remains a very popular activity at various celebrations and perhaps now only inadvertently represents the greater struggles in life that are beyond just breaking the piñata—the overcoming of evil by good.

The eventual breaking of the Piñata by one, is accomplished by the efforts of many in a process that weakens the barriers to its sweet treasures that are available to all.

1
MIGUEL

Who and What Am I?

The value of identity, of course, is that so often with it comes purpose.

—Richard Grant

The quotation that I use to introduce myself in this, the first chapter of my story, once greatly intrigued me. It is not particularly profound, but when I first read it, it triggered something within me. I knew that it held significant truth for me, as it does for each of us. However, at the time I did not then fully appreciate the causes of our changing nature and beliefs and how these serve to shape our individual and collective identities and purposes. Nor did I clearly see how these causes are interrelated in a struggle between our inner life and our life in the world of other people and events. I have become aware of what, for me, was once a great paradox: that in our search for identity and purpose, we are ultimately alone but intrinsically interrelated and interdependent upon one another. It is in this seemingly paradoxical situation that we find authentic identity and a more comfortable sense of being. It is within this paradox that we find the vision, courage, and strength to shape and practice our purpose with action.

My name is Juan Miguel Soto Rios. My family and friends call me Miguel. I am the president of Mexico—the United Mexican States. I am in the last few months of my *sexenio*—the single-term, six-year period that one is allowed to be president under our constitution. I can never run for the presidency of our great country again. There is something about this that makes a review of my efforts and non-efforts as president seem so very final in terms of personal and political accomplishments. This thought has been much in my mind as my term comes to an end. I will never again have the same opportunity to use or misuse the great power that the office of the presidency permits. I wonder how, and if, I have fulfilled my oath of office and *"...with loyalty and patriotism, in all my actions, looked after the good and prosperity of the Union."* I vowed to do so when I repeated the oath of office. I wonder about this, and although I am told that I have done so by some and that I have not done so by others, I think that only time will tell. In any case, I want to write something of my time in office and the great struggle that I have had to find some kind of peaceful satisfaction as a person and as president.

As I reflect upon the events that have occurred during the past six years, I find that I lack the words to fully capture and describe the significance of my discoveries and the great challenges that I have encountered. I am reminded of the profound suffering that comes with transformational effort. I am also reminded of and supported by the great joy that comes in facing the challenge to change. I hope that you will find my inadequate description of these intriguing events and their outcomes not only of great interest, but also of great benefit and in support of your particular journey.

I have been encouraged to write about the few short years of my presidency by my greatest teacher, my wife, María, and by a few friends, as well as others who are my teachers, whom I will tell you about. I have been encouraged to address my thoughts not only to Mexicans, but also to an audience beyond, in the belief that certain events paralleled something very important that is happening globally.

At one time, I simply thought that this was the age-old individual search for meaning, but I now see that it was related to the illusion that what we do individually is somehow quite separate from the thoughts and actions of others. I simply thought that my recounting of this may help others in some small way to reflect upon life and perhaps offer some insight into how we live our lives. However, I now see, in light of my continuing efforts and experiences, that our lives are so interrelated and so much more dependent upon the lives and actions of all people. These are things that my teachers have demonstrated to me. Their wisdom has taught me a lot, and as I write this I am reminded of something else that they have taught me that I think is worth mentioning here and that I now see as very much related to the recommendation to write something about my time as president. They have taught me that although it is of primary importance what happens on the inside—in our minds—we have often learned to more easily and unfortunately succumb to what happens on the outside—the influence and demands of others. In this way we surrender responsibility and our opportunity to begin to free ourselves from what seems like the tangled web of karma that we find ourselves in. Doing this—succumbing to what happens on the outside, what is around us—can be an impediment, and we thereby run the risk of negating our own happiness and the happiness of others. It takes away from what I have learned is the central purpose of our lives. Thus, I hope that my words here are consequential.

Excerpts from sporadic entries from my personal journal form the basis of what I write here. These significant thoughts triggered memories of what I want to tell you. Some of what I write here reflects the persistent churning of thoughts that are sometimes sparked by these memories, and my words might seem a little like a Picasso painting. I hope the overall result brings a more coherent picture than some of the isolated, conflicting, and individual thoughts. I am writing this account of my time as president, in Spanish, my first language and the language in which I think and primarily function. The many and often conflicting voices of my mind constantly repeat things, but in different ways. This too is reflected in my work here. Although I am told that one needs to ignore many of the divergent and particularly the emotion-laden thoughts that come to us, they have often provided me, in part, a reflective means of discernment in some difficult decision making.

This tale is not just an account of my time as president and the great influence that this has afforded me in my official duties. It is also an account of my personal journey, particularly during my time as president. This time in office gave opportunity for the pursuit of some greater purpose and some greater transformation in my life. My wife, María—María Ángeles Santos Aguilar—has told me all these things many times, but at those times I failed to hear them. The voices and influences of those beyond my inner self have always been very strong in my thoughts and actions. Sometimes the wisdom of the people who are closest to us is ignored. I know that María, as my first teacher, and others, have taught me to listen, to be mindful, to pay attention to things. They have reminded me not only to keep learning, but to also be heedful of what I already have heard and what I know in my heart of hearts. They have taught me to pay more attention to the lessons that come from the guidance and teachings on the inside.

I have, as we say in Mexico, sixty-three years. How many more I will have, I don't know. I sometimes think that the sixty-three years *have me*—that I am bound by what I have done and not done. I remember too that lost time is never found again, at least not in this life. When I think of my age and the unknown remainder of my life, I think also of my family members and the desire to always have them close and to always know them, in this life and in the next. My wife, María, and I were both born into riches and privilege. Both families have vast land holdings and businesses in Mexico and abroad. My sixty-three years have taught me to remind myself of these things and that I am not an average Mexican. I have been protected from the great disadvantages of material poverty. I was educated to value and protect the lifestyle afforded to the rich and to protect what was seen as the primary source of our power—our material possessions. María and I both trace our ancestors to the foundation of the Republic, which we often call "our beloved country." Both of our families have a history of strong political involvement and reliance on alliances and privileges that come with material riches. We are part of a core group of families who, since our revolution, participate and hold great political influence in the affairs of Mexico.

Growing up in a materially rich Mexican family with strong political alliances, one learns very quickly of a worldview and accompanying behavior that protects the power that these things bring. It is a kind of corruptness that keeps oneself separate from the world but paradoxically aligns them with the whole of society in the false belief that this is an inevitable condition of most of the rich and that it somehow validates the idea that they are entitled to certain rights that others do not have. It is a subtle corruptness that intimidates and influences, not by breaking the law, but by forcing it to bend because of the learned expectations and the material power one has. It is a corruptness that produces a kind of selfishness, and it influences many of the important decisions one must make in the human journey. I have been confronted with this subtle selfishness, and it has brought me great pain; not so much in accepting it intellectually, but in the practical application of counteracting it or even to believe that it exists.

As a politician, I have not been blatantly or illegally corrupt in the way that is so often a part of our political experience in Mexico. I have never knowingly broken any serious law. However, my corruptness, the corruptness of selfishness, which I learned from birth, comes in the influence that I bring in alliances with others and in the influence that I have allowed others to have over me. I know now that this has kept me from authentic leadership—from responding to the needs of people in a way that does not start with protection of myself and protection of the power of the alliances that I have formed in my many years as a politician. I have become increasingly aware, through introspection and the actions of my many teachers, that the protective attitude that is so strongly fostered in rich and powerful people leads to a kind of frustration and anger. We are only aware of this frustration and anger in relation to our experience of conflict with the less powerful, and it is then directed toward those who have less, who then threaten this corruption of selfishness in their calls for equality of opportunity and the enjoyment of full participation. Equality is a value that the rich and powerful, including many politicians, individually and in their collectively partisan actions strongly pretend to promote but know well that it is their first and most powerful enemy.

My frustration and anger, hidden to me at the time, came from this learned value of protection of my wealth and power; I have acquiesced by listening to what I hear instead of what I know. It has greatly hindered my ability to serve my own real needs and the needs of the people of Mexico. This, in part, is what I have learned and what I want to tell you about; not as a confession, but simply as part of what has influenced my inner and outward struggle.

~~~

Although I had met María many times at mutual family gatherings and social outings, we didn't begin a romantic relationship until we were at Harvard in the United States of America, where we both did post-graduate studies. María and I have two children. Even though they are now independent, are successful in their work, and have good marriages—or at least we visualize them as having these things—we think about them and worry about them and their children. Our son, Lalo, and his wife, Malena, have two sons. Our daughter, Maribel, and her husband, Nacho, have two daughters. We love them all very much, and even though we visit regularly, we agree that we now don't really know them as we once did. They have grown away from us in the way that children do, and we miss them and keenly feel the absence of intimacy. They live in different parts of the Republic, and this adds to this feeling of separation. However, the many photographs and brief messages that they send to us, sometimes twice a week, keep us posted, and we look forward to seeing the little smiling faces of our dear *nietos*, our grandchildren. I feel a great sense of responsibility to them, knowing that as their grandparents, they are the heirs to our attitudes and actions in the same way that all children are to all of us. I see in their little faces great beauty, but also a vulnerability that all children share. They are subject to the influences of the sins and the follies of the adult world and their powerful cultural context.

I became president at a time of great turmoil and conflict in Mexico. Turmoil and conflict seemed to be present in the entire world then and still are. The misuse of power and the resulting danger and violence had become so great in Mexico that it had become intrinsic. The news of horrible crimes committed by the drug cartels in their competitive efforts to control the movement of drugs were constantly in our thoughts. It was the focus of daily conversation of all Mexicans. The national and international press was filled with horrific reports and photographs that graphically showed the results of massacres and other related crimes that brought, if not death, unspeakable misery to many people. Many articles and reports in the international press hinted that Mexico was about to become a failed state. Poor versus rich is one of the most significant divisions in our country, yet all Mexicans were reaching a sense of urgency about the situation. They were united—not in many other things, as is the case in Mexico—in anguish and fear that their very lives could be lost or become even more precarious because of the corruption and violence. Many who had more of a global view of the situation were also worried that our beloved country was, in fact, in ruin. The poverty of words written about the horror of the violence in the press gave much, but was in reality only a hint of the extent of the violence and corruption. The horrific photographs that sometimes accompanied the articles in the press and electronic media gave merely a glimpse of the extent of this destructive horror.

Mexicans often use the term *la crisis,* the crisis, to talk about national issues that are adversely affecting our nation. *La crisis* usually refers to an economic difficulty. Like a great plague, *la crisis* of that time was corruption and the many problems, particularly those related to drugs that stemmed from it. It is said that true crisis ends in destruction or death. We were all aware that it was reaching that point. Mexico could not continue as it was, and this was in the daily thoughts and words of all of us. Crisis often demands great change, sometimes for the better, sometimes for worse. Mexico has changed with the various crises, and particularly within the last few years. I also have changed, or perhaps best said, I am keenly aware of the opportunity to be part of a transformative process that I never dreamed possible. For some, it was a nightmare. For me, the process was indeed a nightmare, and I still live in fear because it is not finished and will not finish at the end of my presidency. It perhaps will not end for many years to come, but I will tell you more of this later.

Living with corruption and the resulting violence and fear of violence can affect our expectations. This is very evident in Mexico. The corruption and misuse of power that has invaded every part of life in Mexico has also brought with it the lowering of expectations. Mexicans are courageous people. However, we have become somewhat fearful, or at least guarded, with the thought of change; particularly change aimed at combating the evils in our country. We are afraid of the conflict that this brings because we know that in the interim, it brings greater suffering because of the fierce reaction from the corrupt ones. The evil ones, like the rich and powerful, if threatened, jealously guard their lifestyle, but they do so with such horrible retaliation. In many ways, we have learned to accommodate the corruption because of the fear of personal loss or retaliation. The global view is somewhat lost when our individual lives or the lives of our loved ones are directly threatened.

There are, on the other hand, examples of great courage and assertiveness in combating the evil ones. This is evident in many family situations and in organized activities aimed at combating crime and corruption. I am particularly impressed by many student groups whose activities in this regard are truly admirable and courageous. Many groups of armed civilians have begun to fight against the drug traffickers. In spite of the great fear that they will become politicized, I secretly admire the members of various community groups who have, albeit illegally, organized themselves against the evil ones. Although reluctantly, we began legalizing these groups and attempted to bring some order to the conflict that they had with one another and within their own groups. The Mexican psyche, which has been influenced by a history of domination by others, does not lend itself well to working in groups, apart from family and very close friends. The alliance against the evil ones by the community groups is strong, but not strong enough to prevent the quibbling and conflict inherent in working with one another that is so very strong in Mexico.

I wonder what the greater evil is—the fear and the resulting accommodation of corruption and the acceptance of this intimidated state, or the corruption itself? To combat this dreadful equilibrium is to risk great conflict and suffering from the ensuing violence. This combat sometimes only *alludes* to change. Risking this necessary conflict and violence is often done at great cost. The fear of personal change, for me, somehow parallels this fear of the change we want for Mexico; and this too has played a very significant part in my journey of change. It has also played a part in gaining insight and the development of tentative truths that are in constant flux and change, which I will tell you about.

Much of my quest—my search for and efforts to change—have been about who I am. In a review of what I have written in my journal, I have discovered that this is a very intriguing and complex question, or at least the search is intriguing and complex. The answer in its simplest form, which I tentatively hold, is that I am one who is aware of the immensity of the issues. The focus and intensity of my awareness, as well as the scope, constantly change and include past, present, and possible future events. My words here are an attempt to reiterate what I was aware of during some past events and reflect the changing intensity, scope, and focus of awareness. However, I believe that the essence of these past events is here.

2

STRENGTH IN WEAKNESS

Responding to Life's Challenge

Each one of us requires the spur of insecurity to force us to do our best.

—Harold W. Dodds

It was mid-September. I had just given my first *Informe Presidencial*, the Mexican president's annual State of the Republic speech. The words were still in my mind, and they haunt me as I think about them. I tried desperately to avoid the word *crisis* and to concentrate on the various good things that were happening in the Republic. I included the extraordinary use of force of law to combat the drug cartels and the related corruption, as well as various reforms. Although I thought what we were doing was the right thing, I knew it to be inadequate. We were losing the so-called war on drugs and in some cases exacerbating the horrible effects that this war had on all aspects of Mexican life. We were indeed losing this battle. This was made evident in the horrible effects of the severe retaliation coming from the corrupt and violent cartels—the evil ones.

It was about 7:00 a.m., and I had just finished my customary light breakfast on the patio overlooking the beautiful gardens of what was my temporary home, the presidential residence. I sat quietly, contemplating the heavy day ahead as I gazed at the beauty of the various shades of brilliant green, interrupted only by glimpses of the soldiers, who tried to stay out of sight but whose presence brought some sense of security mixed with the reminder of caution. I was about to savour the rest of my one and only cup of coffee of the day when I was interrupted by José, our household butler, asking pardon for the interruption and telling me that Don Alfredo—Doctor Alfredo Alonso Rodriguez Alfaro, a senator, an old friend, and one of my chief advisors—had just arrived and was urgently asking to see me.

Alfredo is a warrior, but also a constant worrier. He is a true servant of the people of Mexico and often fights with valiant effort to improve the quality of life for all Mexicans. As a worrier, he is one of the few politicians who lies awake at night worrying and praying for a revelation and thinking about what we could do and how we could deal with the mis-developments that come with rapid social change, a growing population of young people without work, the corruption, the drug problem and the related violence, crime, and the dire poverty that is the plight of so many of our fellow Mexicans.

The Mexican economy, as seen within the context of the world's prevailing monetary systems and political structures, was doing well, and this was seen as the one thing that would turn things around. This was constantly cited as a hopeful sign pointing toward the resolution of Mexico's problems. Alfredo and I had had many discussions about this. We came to the hidden conclusion that the problems that exist cannot be dealt with or eliminated within the framework of the present monetary and political systems. We agreed that a new social and economic order was needed. However, we both realized that this kind of thinking would currently be considered anathema by most of our contemporaries, and thus it was indeed a *hidden* conclusion that we held from others.

Alfredo entered with his customary salutation: "Good morning, my president. How are you?" He appeared tense and sounded anxious.

"I'm well, Alfredo," I replied. "What brings you here so early? Have you eaten? Would you like to have some breakfast...some coffee?"

"No, no, Miguel," he said. "I need to talk to you. It is about our plan, *The Secret*. We are in trouble."

The Secret was an informal name that was now in common use in Mexico and around the world. It referred to ongoing extraordinary confidential meetings. It was the somewhat sarcastic name inadvertently given by my wife, María, for the ongoing talks that I had been having for the last few months with a diverse group of countrymen and a few people from around the world. She had sarcastically called the talks *The Secret* because I was reluctant to tell her details of one of the talks. Cristina, one of María's closest friends, repeated this name to the press, and it soon became widespread. Everyone in the country, everyone in the world, was talking about our *secret* meetings and speculating on their outcome. María's comment to Cristina, calling the talks *The Secret*, had protected her from the constant barrage of questions from her friends and others about the talks, but it had created a false idea that the government's secrets were even greater than they were.

The Secret was clearly not an apt name for our meetings, but the name persisted. It was well known that our activity was related to addressing the extraordinary problems with the drug cartels and other dire needs of the people of Mexico. Our activities, apart from some confidential details, were clearly reported in the *Diario Oficial de la Federación,* The Official Journal of the Government, for all to see. The drug cartels and those who mistrust governments and see something sinister behind everything governments do— no matter what—up-played the secret aspect, and ridiculous speculation was rampant about the details. It was rumoured that everyone involved in the talks had taken an oath not to talk about what the real plans were. The most prevalent belief and fear was that Mexico might again become a dictatorship. Even false secrets can cause great harm. Mexico's past has not been free of harsh and destructive dictatorships.

The non-partisan, secret meeting group consisted of politicians from all parties: clerics, business people, rich and poor, peasants, indigenous people, men and women from all the various groups and subcultures of Mexico, and various experts from other countries. Lawyers seemed to be over-represented in the group, but then this seems often to be the case in any official business in Mexico.

The name *The Secret* was in such common use that even Alfredo was now using it. However, his use of this word was a little disconcerting to me as was his apparent sense of urgency. Alfredo was usually very calm. I wondered if he had again been pressured by some of his many political connections about the value of our planning.

I reminded Alfredo of our meeting later that afternoon by somewhat humorously saying, "It's no *secret* that we have a meeting this afternoon, Alfredo. We could talk about it then. What is so urgent, my old friend?"

Alfredo's very serious reply was, "It was reported in today's press that we intend to suspend rights. Have you not seen it? Have you not read the papers today? It is of course a ridiculous lie, but this will cause great concern and could result in violent protests and take away from our good efforts."

I attempted to reassure him and bring him from his somewhat urgent apprehension by saying, "Well, we knew that this might happen, Alfredo. We knew that the speculations would come to the ridiculous. I am not too concerned about it now because after our meeting today, we can announce our plans immediately and dispel the fears. It is a matter of timing. We are ready. I am more concerned about the reaction to our announcement, and as I said, I think we are ready for this now. Our main concern is with following through with our plans, and now that we have been able to agree upon some strategies, the people have a right to know the details of what we are doing. This, as you well know, has been one of the great problems in our country—not letting the people know what we are doing; and they, *and* we, have waited long enough. We can, at long last, reveal to our people what we have been struggling with and what our plan is. We now need to focus on our next step."

"Yes, yes, perhaps you are right," he replied. "I think that sometimes my ambivalence about what is about to happen, what we are about to do, influences my focus." We looked at each other when Alfredo said this. Both of us knew that what we were talking about was fear. Fear dominated the planning from the start. Fear dominated many aspects of life in Mexico at this time, and we were all prone to succumb to it in various ways.

"Well, my old friend," I said, "you are not the only one who is ambivalent about our plan. Remember this—unless there is some kind of divine intervention, we are doing the only thing that will save the Republic from utter destruction. I think that we are all feeling very uneasy about this. I know that I am. I am not as anxious about the plan itself as I am about the opposition we will be faced with, not only from the people of Mexico, but also from many people throughout the whole world. Many people do not fully understand the seriousness of our situation, and they will be concerned about the human rights issues, which we ourselves have been struggling with."

"Alfredo, relax a little," I said, "I think that all is going as well as it can. I have an informal meeting with a few old friends and some business people from Quintana Roo this morning, but I will see you at our meeting here this afternoon. Why don't you stay here until then? Use one of the offices here to attend to any business you need to, and I will see you this afternoon." I turned my gaze toward José, who was removing the breakfast dishes from a side table. José nodded in response to my words: "José and Doña Margarita will see to whatever you need."

Ana Margarita Robles Martínez, affectionately called Doña Margarita, was and still is my personal secretary. María calls Doña Margarita *La Vivicepresidente*, the vice-president. Mexico does not have a vice-presidency, but *I* do, in the person of Margarita. She is a very capable, strong, and organized person who is always ready to manage various situations and advise me on priorities.

Alfredo slowly nodded in agreement and then smiled. This was his attempt to indicate that he was feeling a little more comfortable and that he would remain and then attend the meeting this afternoon.

My response to Alfredo's fears did not truly reflect the extent of my own inner anxiety and fear at that time. I was, in fact, in a panic and had been for several days. The press is very strong in Mexico. In a recent somewhat restrained attack on the drug cartels, because of fear of additional and more violent retaliation, the press had instead been bombarding the government with confrontations. I knew that any negative speculation in the press would soon turn into pressure and anger from many segments of Mexican society. The people of Mexico, like others who have had a history of suppression, sometimes explode with anger, which quickly spreads into the streets and causes great damage. I wondered what damage any information it presented would cause if it were not dealt with immediately.

My fear that the plan itself might bring open revolt was so strong in my mind that I again and again, in a compulsive manner, went over the explanation that I would give in tomorrow's announcement of the plan. I was hoping that this announcement, in addition to bringing some sense of hope and calm, would also halt Alfredo's expressed fear of impending violent protests.

As I left the room to prepare for the 9:00 a.m. meeting with the representatives from Quintana Roo and *The Secret* meeting in the afternoon, I looked at Alfredo and slowly said, "*Estás en tu casa*—you are in your house, make yourself at home. Whatever you need, just ask José or Doña Margarita. I will see you in the meeting." I wanted the tone of my voice to say, "Relax, all will be well," but I saw that it had failed to do so. Alfredo's usual calm predisposition had been influenced by something apart from the press, something that he was not telling me about.

As I headed toward my office, an overwhelming feeling of weakness, triggered by Alfredo's concerns, overcame me. It was a familiar sensation. It often preceded intense feelings of inadequacy that had plagued me all my life. I was seen as an assertive and strong person, but this hidden side was ever present to me. I was so proud and happy to be president, but at times like this I wondered if it was an impossible job that only a fool would want. How would *this* fool speak with assurance to make the dreaded "Announcement to the People of Mexico"? It was at times like this that my Catholic upbringing, which somehow often magically dealt well with despair, came to the fore, and I uttered an internal, "Lord, be merciful to us. Holy Virgin, pray for us!".

In spite of the recurring and painful feelings of inadequacy and the many fears that plagued me, I had somehow managed to face and meet the many challenges that my life had presented to me. It was a constant battle, but I recognized this effort in myself as strength. I also saw and admired this in others who, in a world gone mad, somehow continued to face the difficult issues of life and carry on.

~~~

My mother was a harsh and insensitive tyrant. My father was the opposite: overindulgent and weak. Although our parents both loved us very much, my brother Diego and I had been greatly affected by the destructive dichotomy of our parents' actions. We had managed to benefit from the love and advice of many other family members, friends, teachers, clerics, and others and to cope relatively well with the damage that had been unintentionally done to us by our parents—well enough to be very successful in our professional lives and in personal relationships. Both of us have strong and mutually supportive marriages and strong and supportive friendships. Finding comfort in our inner lives was, however, quite another issue.

María and I are celebrating twenty-eight years of marriage. María is a strong, sensitive, and supportive person. In a recent conversation, in recognition of my painful feelings of inadequacy, she told me that like Mexico, with its many diverse and critical problems, I was "at war" with myself. She added, "We are all at war with ourselves in some way and we are all inadequate in some respects." I remember forcing a smile at her rather clumsy attempt to comfort me with her modification of her observation of my war with myself.

My thoughts went back to this analogy many times in the following days and continued to do so, particularly in times of personal struggle or when dealing with state issues. I was, at first, very uncomfortable with this analogy and that it came to mind in times of stress. However, I began to affirm the depth of what it meant, and I began also to find it useful, even comforting. It brought the reminder to think in terms of strategies and tactics—to take action and move onward.

I often make little *jokes* to myself. It is one of a few tactics that I use to help me put things into perspective and relieve some of the anxiety that I feel when dealing with difficult issues. After an anguishing attempt to concentrate and prepare for what lay ahead in the day, I walked toward the 9:00 meeting and jokingly told myself that if I could deal with the very aggressive stance of the people from Quintana Roo, I could deal with any reaction to the announcement of any plan to the people of Mexico and the world. The independent and aggressive behavior ascribed to the people of the Yucatan Peninsula was one of the many exaggerated personality traits that Mexicans ascribe to one another of various regions. This joke brought renewed confidence to me, and as president of all Mexico, I walked, head held high, with great bravado but without much internal confidence, into the meeting room.

I was warmly greeted and felt uplifted by the familiar and friendly faces. I took comfort in the thought that I could now leave fear and anxiety behind for a short time and focus on the issues at hand in the meeting. And I did just that.

The meeting went very well, and I was glad to give them assurance of advocacy for some of their concerns related to the promotion of tourism and issues associated with the individual needs of this unique region of the Republic. Many Yucatecans refer to the rest of the country as *México*, as if they were not really a part of it.

Walking back to my office, I remember reflecting upon the meeting and my pleasure at seeing some old friends whose positive and supportive attitude toward me was uplifting. I hoped that the positive feelings that I experienced would be carried into this afternoon's meeting and replace some of the fear that was always at the background of the planning in these sessions. I was, however, conscious that my fears and insecurities kept me looking for answers and doing what I thought was my best in all that I did. That afternoon's meeting was to be the last *secret* meeting before I would announce to the Mexican people the plan that was intended to drastically change the way our government would deal with corruption, poverty, and crime in general, but especially the drug problem, as well as all the evils associated with it. It would drastically change the lives of many Mexicans—and any hint of change, within the culture of fear that dominated the country at that time, was suspect and usually rejected out of hand. This was the great challenge I faced. "Lord, have mercy! Holy virgin, pray for me!"

3

THE SECRET MEETING

The Difficult Context of Change

> *Nothing goes so quickly as yesterday's vision of the future.*
> —Anonymous

I walked into the afternoon meeting still carrying the positive feelings with which I left the morning meeting. My vision of what Mexico could become was strong in my mind.

That vision was very quickly shredded and taken from me in the meeting. It very quickly vanished and was replaced with what seemed like a thick grey fog. The positive feelings that I had had were replaced with feelings that I could not clearly identify. They seemed like a mixture of surprise, anguish, and disbelief. The meeting was a complete and unexpected disaster. I was dumbfounded.

Member after member voted to suspend the plans, to end our sessions, and to have no further discussions. Many indicated support for what the government was currently doing and even praised the current efforts as being adequate—but clearly saying that they would not continue to be part of any *secret* group. Only three of the twenty-eight people had defended my plea to continue with what we were doing and to announce the implementation of our plans. Only Alfredo, Don Alberto Rodríguez Robles (a retired Spanish

Supreme Court judge, who was a nationalized Mexican), and Alfonso Mario Xaxalpa y Xaxalpa (a valued friend and respected indigenous leader) wanted to proceed.

I walked out of the meeting with feelings that I could not clearly identify, but certainly despair and anger. Conflict and disagreements are part of politics, and I had indeed met with an abundance of these in the first few months of my presidency. However, this was different. It was, I thought, clear that this effort was to be the hallmark of my presidency. What had gone wrong? Months of planning and extraordinary efforts were dissolved in an hour! The feelings of surprise, anguish, and disbelief quickly turned into an overwhelming feeling of not only despair and anger, but also of defeat. The feeling of defeat came because this effort was what I believed would have been the greatest accomplishments of my presidency, and this possibility had just been destroyed by the long-reaching arm, with its threats and promises, of the evil ones.

I initially thought that this great change in the minds of so many of the delegates was simply the action of the destructive force of fear. However, had fear alone very rapidly ruined months of planning—planning what I was convinced would turn things around and improve the quality of life for so many? Perhaps it was in fact a clear indication that I had lost the support and confidence of so many, including many who held powerful positions in the party and in various other sectors in the country. Had our efforts brought forth menacing issues of my presidency that were obviously looming behind the scenes and of which I was unaware? What had brought about this very abrupt change of mind and effort?

I continued to explore this in my mind. I returned to my office and found that it was difficult to clearly remember the specifics of what exactly had happened in the meeting—what exactly each person had said. What came to mind was only the issue of the potential reaction of anger and fear of the people of Mexico to our plan. However, this aspect had been clearly dealt with in many sessions. The horrible increase in violence by the drug cartels—which was a certainty—the political opposition, and the real possibility of mass revolt had also been thoroughly and clearly taken into account and included in our plans. The extraordinary measures would have been unfolded little by little, and there had been clear agreement that what we were doing was indeed risky, but necessary. The resulting conflict had been cited, and there had been a clear resolve to continue in spite of certain risks and opposition. Something else had happening here—something more sinister and deceptive.

The very real possibility of strong opposition from the various sources had been discussed in detail. The threat of violence, particularly from the drug cartels was a given, as was the hostility from the political opposition. The previous discussion about the reaction to the political opposition and the possibility of mass revolt had ended with my old friend Cardinal Contreras, who held great power in Mexico and who had been a part of the secret meetings from the start, saying, "Drastic problems require drastic measures…we must proceed." This seemed to put a seal on planned action and halt any further discussion of opposition. However, in the meeting, he was now vehemently arguing against the plans.

As I sat with all these muddled and confused thoughts, my mind was bombarded with many thoughts related to the needs of the people: the dire poverty, greed, corruption, and drug violence and the plans to combat these things. My thoughts always lead me to haunting faces of those affected by these things: the faces of men, women, and children who live with the horrible consequences of corrupt behavior. I saw these faces in my mind, these haunting faces that reminded me of the suffering of so many. I went into the meeting thinking of these faces and with hope of changing things for them. I also saw the faces of those who smugly live with greed and selfishness and who are complicit either by their destructive actions or by inaction in compromising the lives of so many. I also brought *these* faces to the meeting. I was keenly aware that the faces of greed and selfishness were the faces that needed to change first, if the lives of the less powerful were to change. I now saw these faces in the men and women that I had been working with in our secret meetings for the past year. They were, like so many good people in Mexico, influenced not by fear of social change, but by their own personal selfish fears that made them succumb to the influence of the evil ones. I wondered just what promises and threats had been made. I wondered too just how much money had changed hands. I also speculated on what pressures, enticements, and threats Alfredo, Don Alberto, and Alfonso Mario Xaxalpa had been subjected to. I wondered too if they were living with added fear for their lives and the lives of their family members. The anguish that I felt at this moment was almost unbearable. What were their feelings?

I contemplated the thought that the anguish and disappointment that I felt because of what happened in the meeting was also just as much a reaction to a personal political loss, and I wondered if doing the right thing was parallel to my political aspirations. These thoughts would eventually lead the way to an even greater and more important issue in my life. In the meantime, I was faced with feelings of hurt and rejection but also feelings of determination to carry on. It was a kind of false determination and artificial optimism that is often reinforced by the party politicians who surround their leaders and urge them on, often to repeat failed agendas and plans that only *appear* to be successful. In spite of the months of planning together in our meetings, those who were involved from my cabinet ignored what they clearly saw as my disappointment. They had assured me of their support, praising current plans and urging me to continue with what we were doing to deal with the issues that faced us. At the time, I did not see their stance for what it truly was: intellectual dishonesty and deceit based upon fear and perhaps the monetary gains that come with corruption.

In politics, it is not always the emperor who wears no clothes. It is often the politician's advisors and cronies who seek to share in the power. Their delusions are highly contagious and readily shared. At this point, I was, as so many of us are, more influenced by what happens around us and not by what happens within us. I somehow pretended to succumb to the false praise with a kind of artificial determination to carry on in the pretence that we were already doing what was right for the people of Mexico.

Upon the advice of those who surrounded me and appeared to protect me from the truth at that time, I would make a public announcement. I would inform the Mexican people that we had suspended the talks. I would remind the nation of the adequacy and effectiveness of the current measures that our government was taking to deal with the extraordinary problems. I would only later see that this too was part of the plan that had been forced upon those who had so drastically changed their minds about the plans we had in the secret meetings. I had clearly been deceived by many whom I trusted the most and upon whom I had relied. I too was deceptive. I too was lying. It was all wrong. We were not doing what needed to be done. This was, as is often the case in politics, only an issue that was brought to the fore by those suffering from our inadequate leadership and corruption of personal values. I attempted to bury, as I had done many times in the past, the vision of the haunting faces of Mexicans, the haunting faces who were at this moment suffering, not only from the corruption of our actions, but from another corrupt and tyrannical deceit that they were not even aware of.

The Mexican presidency has sometimes been described as an absolute monarchy, indicating the great powers that the president has. Although our system does allow for this and a president can act in what seems like a dictatorial way, the use of this power or the misuse of this power has often been seen as a great strength instead of a great weakness. It ultimately restricts true growth and development. Consultation beyond one's party or social group in given situations is simply not done. It is often seen not only as a weakness, but also as putting oneself and others in a vulnerable position where they might well be seen as being wrong. Vulnerability is a fear deeply rooted in the psyche of Mexicans, as is the fear of being humiliated and losing face.

Many of our leaders have acted with great authority, and some have been ruthless in imposing their ideas without listening to others. These leaders have, in many cases, had fanatic followers who were addicted to these messianic figures who were ruthless in their use of power.

The recent events have given me some greater awareness of my tendency to act in a way that gives some value to consultation and consideration of others' views, in spite of not always acting upon this value. I wonder if this has been too evident in my actions as president. I wondered too if my formation of a bipartisan group made up of people from various levels of society was seen as a great weakness that might well compromise the use of political power. However, it may well have been seen as a great *strength* by the drug cartels—the evil ones. Were the secret meetings doomed from the start? Have I been used as a sort of puppet or taken advantage of by my supporters who have hidden agendas? I hope not. I hope that there is a growing acceptance of the value of consultation beyond the ranks in politics. I hope that it is evident to others that powerful politicians and so-called capitalists have eliminated much of this aspect from what, in name only, are called democracies around the world. It is similar to the worship within belief systems that are almost devoid of teaching individual transformation. We have come to value our democratic systems only because they bear the name *democratic*. They have lost the power to transform society and improve the quality of the lives of people. We have come to admire belief, but we have lost the will to practically apply it because of our selfish fears.

I would carry on. I would make the announcement of the suspension of the talks. I would play the part I was expected to play. However, this experience of what I thought was failure stirred up an old desire to pursue idealistic goals that I had thought were gone. Although nebulous, I felt a strange hopefulness that I was embarking upon something far more important. I held vague thoughts of optimism that I then superficially identified as simply magical thinking. One cannot change the awesome power of corruption and a system that does not, by its practical application, encourage the development of ethics and wisdom but seeks to simply control and encourage individual competition. It is a system that encourages deviant alliances, and I must, I told myself, somehow again accept this reality as I had done in the past. Any effort to combat or change any of this, I remember thinking, would only take away from the energy of the good efforts that I have made while operating within this structure, within this tangled web of politics that we are all caught up in.

Partisan political action, carried forth and fostered, particularly from the intense competition and the attainment of power by being on the winning side, brings with it a kind of bravado and an attitude of righteousness. Although parties do not claim absolute truths, we sometimes act as if we are dealing with things of this nature. It is so easy to be caught up in this and forget that we are not gods and that we are vulnerable to the same tentative truths that all humans live with. It is this tentative truth that is reflected in what is seen as the failure of the leaders of the world to respond to the needs of their people. Although there are varying degrees of some kind of consultation within the various systems of government, the basic action of governments seems usually to be based on or influenced primarily by material gain and laws that primarily sanction existing economic relationships that serve the rich and powerful. I feel caught up in this oligarchic system and sometimes wonder how I ever got here, but I know quite well how I got here. How very tentative indeed are our beliefs and convictions. How much we can change with age and a little experience! However, we seem to cling to the same behavior and remain in the false security of beliefs and values that are reinforced by our own thoughts and also by the thoughts of other people who have the same insecurities. We cling to what is more comfortable. We cling to what we know intellectually is wrong. We succumb to our emotional desires, which seem to hold us from the risk of new insights we might gain and which might help us to truly develop.

The failure of the secret meetings held a secret success. Somewhere within the compulsive and confused thoughts that the outcome had brought to me was a sense of greater resolve to do something. It was very small and very elusive, but it held me from remaining in despair and defeat. It was enough resolve to do this but still retain the anger, an anger that somehow I knew would prompt me to continue not only in thought, but also in some kind of action. I wondered how such a small hope could bring such a strong but strange sense of security, but it did, and I was grateful. I was grateful to continue to walk in the dark with only hopefulness for a guide.

~~~

María convinced me that I needed a break from politics for a while. "I will go with you. I need a break too," she said. We would go to the ranch for a week. I would make a public announcement about the suspension of the meetings and then go. Although María listened closely to my attempts to explore my concerns about what had happened in the meeting, she consistently responded to each explanation by saying, "You need a break!"

As the intensity of my appeal to her to explore the situation heightened, I became very anxious, almost screaming at her because of her refusal to explore the details. I became aware that I did indeed need some time away. Only after my eventual response to her, saying, "I'm sorry, you are right, María, I do need to get away for a while" was I able to relax. This admittance, this verbal expression of my need, brought a barrage of conflicting thoughts. Relaxing with these myriad thoughts, in the end, brought me to the realization—a reminder really, that my life was more than being president. Not that this was any less important than anything else, but that I had become not so much obsessed with my job, but caught up in the pressure and stress that it brings, and I was beginning to exclude the practical application of the principle of interrelatedness. I was losing perspective. Although *thinking* at such stressful times seemed to be my worst enemy, I did indeed need to think about this.

The family ranch was a refuge for us, and the decision to go—in spite of the ambivalence centred in the crisis of deception that I had experienced, the threat this presented to my presidency and to any meaningful continuation in politics—did in fact trigger a great sense of relief. I was also supported by the strange sense of security that I had experienced in an even more elusive sense of resolve to carry on. I imagined myself sitting outside sipping my one cup of coffee in the very quiet and peacefulness of the mornings at the ranch. I also saw myself wandering about the place, walking along the river, talking to people in the nearby village, and eating tacos at the small taco stand next to the old colonial-era village church. I enthusiastically embraced the decision to go to the ranch with these thoughts. They had brought me from great conflict and anguish to a relative but very tentative sense of peace.

The decision to leave the pressing problems, or at least to deal with them from afar, along with the thoughts of the deception by many who had enthusiastically supported my plans, also brought to me a sense of being very alone, which arose not so much from the deceit but from the aggregate of the many factors in a system that held us captive to its corruption for so long. Alone was where I knew that I must be for a while. Some time at the ranch might provide this, as well as a new point where I could continue or start anew with a healthier perspective on things, and give time for further consideration of that very small and elusive sense of security and resolve that somehow managed to linger in my thoughts.

4
REFUGE

Retreat, Solitude, and Insight

The last of the human freedoms is to choose one's attitude in any given set of circumstances, to choose one's own way.
—Victor Frankel

The small, elusive sense of security and resolve that I held became more evident and grew with my visit to the ranch. My retreat to Santa Rosa was a very great gift. What I expected to be only a temporary escape from the turmoil and stress was much more than this. It was a move toward my personal liberation and a clearer view of my presidency. I gained a better idea of what I had set aside to act the role of president and how taking time to reflect upon my life had affected me. I also gained a more evolved idea of what I must do to help liberate the people of Mexico from the tyranny of evil, the tyranny of the evil ones who had forgotten or had never learned how to live. As I write this, it all sounds very dramatic. How could my thoughts change so dramatically? Nothing ever really unfolds so easily and clearly to bring such vivid insights into life's priorities, but my words express the surprise of even a small change, which in this case was very significant to me. The retreat brought a silence in which I was able to relax and reflect upon what I had heard from others who had no personal agenda related to political gain, survival, or manipulation. It reminded me of a time when I had little influence, responsibility, or power over collective action. In my rise to the presidency, I had lost some autonomy and independence as I succumbed to the pressures of partisan politics and the force and influence of additional material power.

We are all teachers to one another, and I was reminded of this very important fact in my encounters with my own teachers, the people with whom I met during my retreat to the ranch.

Just before the announcement that we had suspended the secret meeting talks, there was another report of a horrific massacre in a northern border city, and this held the attention of the press for several days. It also kept it away from speculation and criticism of what I thought would be a very negative reaction to the announcement of the suspension of the talks. However, in any case, and as in all cases of such horrible news, this latest violent act added to my underlying and pervasive preoccupation with the drug-related problems and was a reminder of the failure of the great effort and hope that I had put into the secret meetings. It also reminded me that I could in no way easily erase the events of the last secret meeting from my mind in a short respite at the ranch. In spite of this, I had resolved to go to the ranch to retreat from some of the turmoil, not really knowing how I would do this.

Santa Rosa, our family ranch or hacienda, is a large estate. It has changed hands a few times since the colonial era, when it was given to my family by the Spanish crown. However, it always came back to us. It is still a productive farm, and we are fortunate to have a loyal and dedicated staff to operate this very special place. It is adjacent to an ancient village that has its own interesting history. Santa Rosa is a beautiful and magical place of great natural beauty and wonderful old stone buildings that have been kept in excellent condition. It has remained a place for important family events and gatherings. No family members live there now. It has become mostly a place for weekend trips and vacations, a refuge and retreat from the world of stress and pressure. Family members and a few friends use Santa Rosa as a metaphor for peace, rest, recuperation, insight, and unity. Our times at Santa Rosa often bring us to useful perspectives and a sense of support and insight that are somehow very strongly aligned to our inner life and sense of good purpose.

Apart from the permanent staff members, María and I were the only family members at Santa Rosa for the two weeks that we spent there. My brother, Diego, and Marta Ana usually came every weekend but had recently been unable to come because of commitment priorities. I was looking forward to talking to Diego, and his absence and my desire to talk to him, as I usually did when we were at Santa Rosa together, cued a greater realization of the need to explore what were, at that time, my greatest concerns and challenges.

Family members would use our time together at Santa Rosa to share with and support one another. I would miss this mutually supportive interchange. We often remarked, after a visit to the ranch, that we found new insights into life's priorities because of our close family discussions. With Diego's absence, I would not think of looking to others for this supportive interaction in my time at the ranch, but it would nevertheless come to me in other unexpected ways.

After two days of sleeping in, horseback riding, eating slowly, and other, seemingly rare relaxing activities, María and I decided to wander over to Santa Clara de Las Flores, the little nearby village. We had a wonderful relaxing time, and we were reminded that these small, colourful, and relaxing places still held many simpler and easier ways of life in spite of the world gone mad about them. I was only reminded of this other world as I caught glimpses of the ever-present security guards who followed us and watched over us and who tried to blend in when we reached the village but could not in such a small place. We were glad to meet and exchange well-wishes with old friends and acquaintances in Santa Clara de Las Flores. I missed this kind of interaction with people, and I felt uplifted and humbled to again talk with people whom I fondly remembered as friends and acquaintances and with whom I felt no pressure to perform in some way, either as their president or friend.

Although I resisted at first—clinging to the idea that I must be alone for a while—my visit to the village, and María, convinced me that it would be good to have some friends for dinner while we were at the ranch. We decided to invite our old friends Father Antonio, Bud and Stella, and Héctor and Isabel, but on three separate occasions. I am so glad that I agreed with María to invite them. It was indeed a good thing to do. Each visit was like a great gift and provided me with reminders of things that had not been included in my reflections as of late and much more. Each, in fact, gave me a renewed hope in my quest for a better me and a better Mexico and for how I would proceed with my growing sense of resolve.

5
FATHER ANTONIO

A Witness to Love

> *How far that little candle throws his beams!*
> *So shines a good deed in a weary world.*
> —William Shakespeare, *The Merchant of Venice*

Our first guest at Santa Rosa was Father Antonio, or Padre Toñio, as we affectionately called him, who was now in his eighties. He has been the parish priest at San Martín de Pores Church in the village since his ordination. He was one of the people who had greatly helped Diego and me to meet the challenges of our rather difficult early family life. He remains a kind and generous man, and I greatly respect and care for him. I was eagerly looking forward to seeing him.

I had not seen Padre for a long time, his presence brought back memories of family, friends, events of my childhood and youth, and also of the strong beliefs that I once held, or thought that I held. Upon seeing him again, much older, smaller, stooped, wrinkled, and now frail, I felt a lot of gratitude for the friendship and support that he had given to our family. Father was eager to hear what was happening with family and old friends and fondly remembered the strong relationship he had with my parents and grandparents. He was also very anxious to share the fact that he was very keenly affected by what was currently happening in Mexico and by the suffering that many Mexicans were currently experiencing. Our conversations centred on these things.

Padre was accustomed to giving advice. He was eager to comment on what I might do, as president, to alleviate the suffering. We were so happy to be with him and to have a dialogue with him, and as I listened to him and some of his ideas and thoughts, I was reminded of how compassionate and kind he truly was in the expression of his desires for others. I saw too, however, how very much I had moved away from the common beliefs of many, if not most, Mexican Catholics. However, I had not had occasion to clarify my thoughts about God or the church, and I thought that it might be important to do this. I had had the usual discussions about the church and its role in our society. I had had a lot of contact with various organizations and clerics in the church and had taken into account the changing influence on the people of Mexico of not only Catholicism but now the rising growth of various Protestant sects, atheism, and such things as *La Santa Muerte*—the veneration of the personification of death. However, I had never really taken time to clarify my own beliefs.

It appeared to me that Padre Toñio's experience had kept him in a belief system that was heavily reliant upon the Virgin, God, and various saints. The Virgin, Our Lady of Guadalupe, was the first one to appeal to for help. It was a belief system that heavily relied upon these powers to break natural law and solve whatever problems were at hand. Although I thought that this rarely happened, the belief was still very strong, or perhaps it was simply that many could not see any alternative. Father also stressed his belief in the importance of accepting the dogma of the church and in following what the church teaches. He saw this as the key to the resolution of all personal and collective problems. This simplistic view had served him well, and it seemed that this, and whatever else he practiced, had been a transformative process for him. We used to say that Padre was *nació bueno,* born good, and that he didn't need to work at it. In any case, the church offered me and many others very little in terms of promoting personal transformation as opposed to blindly, and sometimes fearfully, conforming to the teachings. People had been greatly affected by these teachings, but now many only paid lip service to them, in a kind of pretense and in social custom strongly related to family. For many Mexicans, religion and the cultural practices that have evolved around Mexican Catholic practice were almost devoid of a clear spiritual aspect. I remember once hearing a priest say that many Mexicans hang rosaries from the rear-view mirrors of their vehicles thinking that their prime purpose was to keep evil spirits away. He went on to say that even though they knew it did not *work* without prayer or affirmation, they kept them there out of habit but without any thought at all, let alone prayer or affirmation.

The church has influenced Mexicans to be over-reliant upon saviours and magic—to some extent, to be reliant upon others to solve their problems. This dependency upon others is part of the complex Mexican personality profile, and it affects all aspects of Mexican life. It has created a kind of magical thinking that extends, in some cases, even to drug lord heroes, dead or alive, who are relied upon to help individuals and their families obtain wealth and security. Mexico is, however, not unique in terms of this dynamic. Religious systems throughout the world seem to have created this reliance upon their beliefs and have often been threatened by individual transformation that questions their salvific messages and control.

As we talked to Padre Toño, my mind was flooded with thoughts that were cued by what he was saying. The plans that we were ready to announce as a result of the secret meetings essentially consisted of more force and increased use of military control and laws that would greatly restrict and control commerce and monetary systems. Part of the plan also included a proposal for the widespread use of penal colonies, similar to the ones that we have at Islas Marías, off our Pacific coast. The Mexican people had not been directly involved in the planning of these things. Although we attempted to have representation from various parts of the population, there had been no direct consultation. This is often the case in planning and law making. We are not ancient Greece. However, I could not help thinking that we must find a way to motivate and include Mexicans to a greater degree. It occurred to me that the government sometimes does exactly what the church has done in terms of decision making and acts as a kind of saviour of the people, creating a false dependency. We were also fearful of independent transformation and action. I wondered if our ambivalent decision to officially recognize and sanction some activities of the so-called vigilante groups, the *Autodefensas*, was inadvertently the first step in involving the populace to a greater degree. These groups, which were formed outside the law to protect and combat local drug cartels, were given our reluctant and informal sanction primarily because we were fearful of the loss of support and reprisals from the local people who support their actions. I found myself looking forward to having time to further explore these thoughts. I knew that the issues related to these things were important components of authentic social and political development.

Romero, one of our security personnel, a giant man who never smiled and was always very abrupt with everyone, was waiting for Padre at one of our vehicles, to drive him back to the parish after his visit. As I walked with Padre to the car, Romero, who obviously knew Padre, approached and directed us to the car with very great respect and a smiling face. I did not recognize *this* Romero. It was almost disconcerting to see this change in his behavior.

I later asked Romero, "Have you known Father Antonio for a long time?"

"Oh yes," he replied, "I have known him for a long time, my president."

His tone, perhaps encouraged by my inquisitive look, seemed to indicate his desire to explain, and I prompted this with an inquisitive, "Oh?"

He continued to tell me about his relationship with Padre: "Yes, my president, Father Antonio is like our *Santo Patrón*, our patron saint. My wife is from a small village in Jalisco. Many years ago, when she was just a child, after several weeks of rain, a mudslide took five lives and left forty-three others without even a drop of water to drink. After hearing that a political conflict, really a familial conflict, prevented the governor from helping the village, Father Antonio came with others from his parish to literally save the lives of forty-three villagers. I would not have the great gift of my Graciela and my two sons if it were not for Padre. We all love him, my president. Every year 204 of us go to Santo Tomás Abajo—that is the name of my Graciela's village—to honour Father Antonio and the holy Virgin who brought him to save the village so many years ago."

He continued after a pause, saying, "Father Antonio was not able to come this year. We missed him so much. I was so glad to see him now. Thank you so much, my president."

I was surprised at Romero's many words and the enthusiasm with which he spoke about Padre. I was reminded of the great importance and positive influence of goodwill and the very supportive presence of Father Antonio and of so many other Mexicans who encourage us in our lives. I also wondered about the many people who had been affected by Padre's quiet, compassionate way.

After making an arrangement for Padre to come to Santa Rosa the following week to say mass in our private chapel, we bid each other goodnight, and he promised the support of his prayers. As I walked back, I thought of the great benefit of having Padre come to say his mass, "For the resolution of the crisis," as he said. We would invite the locals, and we would be uplifted by this very positive social action. I also was reminded not to confuse goodwill and encouragement with faith. Faith alone, to me, seems useless and offers no real solution except perhaps for a brief retreat from the challenge of testing our belief in actions—the actions that serve to improve the quality of our lives and not bind us to belief without practical application.

My thoughts about my discussions with Father Antonio brought me reminders of the importance of remembering that in spite of whatever belief or disbelief we profess to have, the thing that really matters is how we treat one another and how we respond in unity with our common basic ideas of justice and compassion. I remember thinking that this is at the core of our efforts to live in peace with one another and that by looking to dogma, we might compromise this.

As a young person, I often felt guilty about discussions that I had with Padre, particularly when he was giving advice or encouragement. He would include in his advice and encouragement things such as prayer, the Virgin, the saints, God, and other religious things. I remember interpreting what he was saying subjectively and rejecting some good advice out of hand simply because of the language he used. As I talked to him recently at Santa Rosa, I realized that I was able to look beyond the vocabulary he used and glimpse the universal values he expressed. I found this very unifying, and I was grateful for this revelation.

Father's visit also brought me many other things to think about in the following days and greatly influenced some unexpected decisions that I would eventually make. However, an even greater influence, because of his kindness, would manifest itself in the lives of our next guests.

6
BUD AND STELLA

Thriving in Adversity

...suffering produces endurance, and endurance produces character, and character produces hope.
—Romans 5:3-4

Bud and Stella are friends from our undergraduate days. Stella—Estella María García Durán—was a student at the University of Guadalajara where María and I both did our undergraduate studies. Bud—Gordon Smart—met her at a party while he was on a student exchange trip. They fell in love upon their first meeting. Both were frequent visitors to Santa Rosa, and when my parents invited them to have their wedding there, they immediately accepted and were married in our chapel shortly after Stella's graduation. Padre Toñio, who knew Stella's family, was very glad to witness their wedding. They moved to the US after they were married. Bud continued his graduate studies and Stella started to work as a professor of Hispanic Literature.

We had kept in touch with our old friends over the years, but only with brief exchanges of greetings and family information. We knew that they were happy in their work. Bud had become a very successful surgeon, and Stella continued to work as a professor and had published many bilingual children's books. We also knew that they had a daughter who was married and that, like us, were very proud and fond of their grandchild. Apart from this, we then knew very little of their lives. We were surprised when we heard of their early retirement. They were both in their early sixties, and both loved their work. We were even more surprised that they had recently chosen to move back to Mexico where they would be away from their daughter and grandchild. However, here they were in Mexico; very close to Santa Rosa in an old colonial-style house near Santa Clara de Las Flores. We wondered how we would presently find them. They were our next guests, and we very much looking forward to seeing them and hearing about their lives.

When we were alerted to their arrival at Santa Rosa, we went to greet them at the main entrance and saw their car coming up the long driveway. As Bud and Stella stepped from the car, María could not contain herself and quietly whispered to me saying, "¡*Dios mío!*"—"Oh my God!" We were shocked at their appearance. They both looked dishevelled and much older than we expected them to appear. Bud and Stella were very handsome people who had always carried themselves with great dignity and composure. This drastic change, in spite of the passage of time and the usual stresses of life, was unusual. Something had obviously gone very wrong. Something *was* wrong! Their appearance and comportment could not possibly result from ordinary living, no matter how stressful it may have been. My wondering what had happened to them turned from curiosity about the years we had not seen them to a dreaded concern for their current well-being.

Bud and Stella were very quick to clearly acknowledge the shock that their appearance held for us and that we had attempted to hide. They were both agitated. "We know we look like hell," Stella said, continuing, "We know you might not want us here."

"Please Stella," Bud said, trying to halt further comments.

I slowly and clearly said to them, "We want you here. Please come in… you are *in your home*."

This was an unusual situation, and Bud acknowledged this by saying that they would like to explain what their situation was and then apologetically said something to the effect that perhaps they shouldn't have come. We assured them that this was not the case, in a clumsy way, attempting to ease the discomfort of the situation. Feeling that we should have known what had happened to them, I said something about our failure and regret for not having kept in touch with them.

As we listened to their account of the events of their lives in the past year, I was astonished. I was shocked. I was greatly disturbed and felt great compassion for them. Bud explained their story, and Stella interjected to add details of a very distressing tale. The vision of Bud and Stella from past times years blurred what I was about to hear. I fought disbelief out of respect for the honesty and frankness in what they related to us.

Bud and Stella's daughter, their son-in-law, and their granddaughter had died within three months of one another. Several months ago, they had been on their way to visit Bud and Stella, and they were involved in a horrible car accident. They were hit by a drunk driver. David, their son-in-law, died in the car. Their daughter, Liz, and their granddaughter, Monica, hung on to life in a hospital for several weeks, but died within three weeks of each other. They never regained consciousness.

David and Liz, we were told, were both highly intelligent, had completed post-graduate studies, and were very successful in their careers. They were both very committed to the service of others and had very strong family values. David was a lawyer, and Liz worked as counsellor in a drug rehabilitation centre. They had a good marriage and were devoted to each other and to their daughter, Monica.

It was so shocking to hear this very sad recollection of events and speculate on the obvious suffering. I cannot now recall all of the words that Bud and Stella had said to convey it. I do remember being very surprised that they were even able to talk about it. There was a kind of serenity about them as they spoke that was very disconcerting. I wondered how, in the face of such horrible suffering, they could even continue to function, and this still remains somewhat of a mystery to me, although they did attempt to explain this along with the other aspects of their great loss.

Bud and Stella told us that quite apart from even functioning in a normal way, they were totally immobilized by their feelings. Both of them had contemplated suicide. Initially they were able to talk to each other about had happened but became so lost in their sorrow that they could not even tolerate discussion with each other, look at each other, or even be in the same room together. They both had what Stella explained was a reactionary anger at everyone and everything, including themselves and each other. Friends and professional colleagues tried to offer support and encouragement, but they were turned away with expressions of horrific anger. Some of Stella's family members came from Mexico and offered to remain after the funerals, but she would not let them. The only person they could tolerate was Lupita, or Guadalupe, their live-in maid.

Lupita had been with them since the birth of Monica, and in their words, she had apparently kept them alive. "She saved our lives," Stella said. Lupita was from Guadalajara. She had worked for Stella's family as a young woman but eventually went to the US, became a resident, and decided to remain. She had intended to return to Mexico and marry her childhood sweetheart, but he married someone else, so she decided to remain in the US.

Her mother, Agustina, had known from Stella's mother that Stella and Bud were looking for a maid, and she suggested that Lupita contact Stella. Bud and Stella were delighted to have her.

"She was one of our family," Bud remarked. "She helped us bring up Liz."

Stella added, "She was like Liz's second mother and a second grandmother to Monica."

In the midst of her own grief and anguish, Lupita had somehow managed to look after Bud and Stella, trying to at least encourage them with activities of daily living. They were unable to work and had remained in the house, barely existing. Apparently Lupita began to despair of being able to help them, to even begin to think of talking or doing something about their grief, which seemed to hold them like prisoners in an abyss. Apart from her prayers, she didn't know what else to do, but she knew that some action was needed.

At that point, Lupita had contacted Padre Toñio. She had remembered that he had intervened with one of her family members in a similar situation. As she spoke on the telephone to him, as she later told Stella, she was thinking that it was a very stupid thing to do. However, she was surprised but very glad that he immediately said that he was coming and would try to help. She later told Stella of her call to Padre, but her gladness quickly turned to fear when she told Stella that he was coming. She had not really expected Padre to even consider coming. Both Bud and Stella became very angry with her, and she became fearful of their reprisals. In spite of this, Padre came within a week, and remained with them for three days. It made things worse for a while, but eventually it changed things around and brought hope and, more importantly, action, and that would bring some sense of comfort to their lives.

I wondered why Padre Toño had not told us about Bud and Stella when he was here. He knew that we were friends. He knew that we were going to be seeing them. We had told him this. I didn't know. I did know that at first, his visit to Bud and Stella was not at all welcome. I also wondered how Padre could even make such a trip. He was in his eighties and very frail. I don't think that he had ever been out of Mexico. I doubt that he even had a passport. How could he even arrange such a visit? "*Dios mio!*" Somehow he had indeed managed to do this, even contemplating the hostility and rejection that he would likely meet from Bud and Stella.

Bud reminded us that they were both atheists and had had very little to do with the church and that it seemed like a grave insult that this priest would interfere in their time of great anguish and grief. "Yes, you are a friend of Stella's family and you witnessed our marriage, but how dare you do this to us. How dare you impose your pious nonsense on us at a time like this?" Bud had apparently repeated this to Padre at the front door when he arrived to see them. However, they did allow him in and became at least civil to him.

That same day, for the first time in many weeks, Bud and Stella ate dinner together, along with Padre. Stella said she felt that in spite of her anguish and hurt, she was uniting with Bud against an intruder by joining him at dinner. However, she said, in a strange way, sitting with Bud and Padre, she began to see that Bud was suffering just as much as she was and she felt great compassion for him. It seemed odd to feel anything beyond her own grief, and this opened a new element in their terrible time of grieving. Bud related that he also felt this. They both seemed to lose some anger and began to relate to Padre in a different way. Although they were unwilling or unable to talk to one another about anything deeper than the food they were eating, they began to feel differently about his visit. His presence somehow enabled them to emotionally include him as a guest who cared for them. Bud and Stella, for the first time in weeks, slept in the same room that night, and they began to talk to each other. They agreed to let Padre talk to them; mostly out of what they felt was pity for an old man who hardly spoke English, coming this far to attempt to console them. This looking beyond themselves was to be the start of a way out for them.

Although they did not go into details of Padre's discussions with them, apart from Bud telling us that Padre never mentioned God, Jesus, or the Virgin, he somehow managed to get Bud and Stella to talk to him about their loss and grief, and he then suggested that they come to Mexico, at least for a few months, where they might begin to heal and also where they could be closer to Stella's family. Lupita was to come with them. At first they were so surprised and shocked by such an audacious suggestion that they immediately rejected it in great anger and even laughed openly at Padre. However, whatever he had said to them, he was somehow able to get them to agree with his plan. They managed to make arrangements, and they left for Mexico within a couple of weeks. Padre told them about the old house near the village. He also told them of the desperate need of the children in an orphanage near where they would be living, and he asked them to consider an invitation to become involved in the work there.

"We really have no idea how this came about—how we were able to make such a decision," Bud said. "We were so dysfunctional, so sad and angry that we hardly could bathe or dress ourselves, let alone plan to move. How could we possibly consider working in an orphanage? We could hardly bear to talk to anyone about the loss of our grandchild. Somehow we just did it. We still don't quite know how we got here. We did, however, feel a great sense of love and acceptance from Padre. Lupita's loving actions, along with Padre's presence and help, were enabling in a way that we just cannot quite understand."

I knew that Bud and Stella were strong, action-oriented people, but it was very difficult to believe that they were able to begin to cope so well after their ordeal. As they were leaving, they talked of going to the orphanage in the morning and how they were looking forward to this and how they went daily. They told us that they were not functioning well but that every day they were feeling a little better; it was healing to be doing something helpful with the children. They were still very much grieving and suffering all kinds of physical and emotional distress. However, they were in fact able to function, even if it was with great sorrow and extraordinary effort. They found that they were able to accept the continued support of Padre Toño and additional help from Stella's sister, who was now in constant contact with them and had visited them several times. Lupita remained their devoted friend and core support. She was also apparently very glad to be back in Mexico.

Bud and Stella's tragedy brought me great sorrow and sadness. Nevertheless, their response to their situation brought me great amazement. I was amazed at the power of love and goodwill. We are often amazed at this power, and perhaps we should not be. It seems to minimize what we know in our heart of hearts. I wondered how I would cope with such a catastrophe and what might bring me some solace. In my official capacity as president, I am often called upon to offer condolences and visit sites where great tragedies have occurred. I was reminded of the great power of compassion, which triggers the enormous strength that we all have, sometimes hidden even from ourselves.

Thinking about this also led me to thoughts of the many people in Mexico suffering the loss of children, parents, friends, and others because of the corruption and drug-related problems. The haunting faces of our people who were greatly suffering in so many ways came to me again and again. I wondered what acts of love and goodwill would help bring them from despair and bring about changes for them, and I wondered too if those who govern them even think in terms of providing them with this love and goodwill. I did not. I did not see this as my responsibility. Yes, I loved my people. I felt great sorrow with their suffering, but these were bound up and hindered by my prime loyalty to my party and in perpetuating a system that deals with problems that threaten the country and its people primarily with the force of arms—with control.

These and other muddled thoughts came to me. I had always known that my attitude and actions were controlled to a great extent by the expectations of other politicians and very successful business people, but I had never seen this as a kind of intellectual dishonesty that kept me from authenticity as a person and as a president. These thoughts confronted me. I knew that the practice of compassion is true and right and that knowledge of this was coupled with a just judgment as to what action I must take to begin to cooperate with this powerful force. My thoughts, expanding as they do, brought me also to what, in the moment, I thought was a dysfunctional place where I was again idealistically dreaming of an ideal world. *I must be practical,* I thought, even in this very tired state, *but are not my thoughts and ponderings simply a part of the dynamic that we are all coming to in our quest for reality, somehow carried along by the action of grace or karma or whatever one sees this as?* I was very tired. I needed to get some sleep.

Stella and Bud's tragedy had greatly affected me. My thoughts would not permit me to escape from myself, but I had to continue my break from the troubles of my job and, for now, bury such thoughts of being a saviour to Mexico, as I was once accused of in one of the secret meetings!

7
HÉCTOR AND ISABEL

The Great Gift of Authentic Teachers

Education is the most powerful weapon which you can use to change the world.
—Nelson Mandela

Héctor and Isabel—Doctor Héctor Guzmán Ruiz and Doctor María Isabel Alfaro Fuentes—have been my friends for many years. They are well-known and very well-respected Mexican educators and authors. He is a professor of psychology and wellness, and she is a professor of anthropology. They both work at the prestigious *El Colegio de México*, in the Federal District, where they also have their principal residence.

El Colegio de México is a university that specializes in teaching and research in the social sciences and humanities. Héctor and Isabel have both worked there for many years. They decided to take a sabbatical year together to write and were spending a lot of their time at Dos Rios, her family's ranch. It is beautiful place and a quiet place to work. The ranch is adjacent to Santa Rosa.

As a child, Isabel spent her holidays at the family ranch, and we became friends. We have kept in contact over the years and have often met with her and Héctor at various family events and other functions. Like so many of my friends, I have not made time to be in contact with or visit them for a long time. While they were at the family ranch, María and I thought that it would be a good opportunity to see them, and they became our third invitees. We were very much looking forward to seeing them.

Reflecting on our time with them, I am reminded that I somewhat compelled them to answer many questions that kept us talking into the early hours of the next day. What would usually end a very enjoyable dinner and discussion carried on for a very long time. María became very tired at midnight, and she excused herself and retired. Héctor, Isabel, and I continued our discussion.

The poverty of words often fails to express what we are really thinking and feeling. It is a rare gift to meet and enjoy the friendship of people with whom one has a real sense of unity in thoughts and feelings, in spite of this limitation of words. Héctor and Isabel are such people. I have always been able to talk to them about anything and feel a great bond and sense of mutual comprehension. It was so good to be with them again and to enjoy meaningful discussions that didn't drift off into orbital dialogues. It was good, too, in a way that was entirely unexpected, but it took me a while to discover the full extent of this.

I have always greatly respected Héctor and Isabel's ideas and found that my discussions with them always brought me to a very contemplative state. I have learned much from them. This visit to Santa Rosa was no exception. My discussion with them brought forth a somewhat strange and very significant confirmation of things that I had been pondering and would, upon greater reflection, eventually bring a kind of affirmation and some greater tentative revelation of what I accept as *my truths*. The confirmation, questioning, or rejection of these tentative truths comes with ongoing experience. My discussion with Héctor and Isabel brought this kind of confirmation. My enquiry about their sabbatical year and their work brought not only some very important reminders of the complexity of human behavior, but also some important reminders of very basic things—things that I needed to hear and that would add to my somewhat compulsive thought process in a search for meaning and practical application.

Héctor and Isabel hold a keen interest in and knowledge of each other's work and professional activities and share many of the same ideas. Their discussions about their then-current writings had brought them to a realization that they were both very interested in bringing together much of what they had studied, taught, and written about in the past, a kind of summary with conclusions about various things in their respective fields. Their discussions led them into talking, about not only the use and implications of their writings, particularly in lecturing on these subjects, but also about an aspect that they found was often a weaker part of their own lectures and writings, perhaps because of the nature of the courses they had taught.

Primarily as teachers, their focus had been on explaining things. Their latest work brought them both to a more global view and discussion that implied a more action-based exploration of what they were researching. Application became their major focus and their intention. Their discussions bought them to the idea of working together and producing a work that would not only enhance understanding of their respective fields and general knowledge but would couple with insight and judgment as to what action should be taken to improve the quality of leadership, particularly in education and politics. This is an aspect of the use of specialized knowledge that is often missing in politics. We are sometimes eager for an explanation of things in order to justify our actions or appease people but fail to practically apply the recommendations of experts, being hemmed in and influenced by our loyalties to parties, lobbyists, and other affiliations. I think that this is generally true in many aspects of our way of dealing with knowledge, belief, and information in western society. We seem to be so preoccupied with explanations of things and articulation of what we believe, as opposed to making our first goal the action itself. The treatment of belief in western society often hinders correct action, or any action at all. We tend to worship belief and put emphasis on belief instead of action.

Isabel was originally working on the history of specific events in Mexican history that had had an extraordinary influence on the process of development of the republic into a modern state. Hector's original work centred on the interrelationship between individual behavior and collective behavior and the effects this has had on Mexican institutions of education and political leadership.

These were not new topics. Many interesting and informative works have been written on these subjects; nor was there anything particularly new in the subject of their combined effort, which was essentially a combination of the two focuses. However, what was new and of great interest to me was their strong focus on recommendations for social change and, in particular, their recommendations on leadership in any field. I was particularly interested to hear what they had to say about political leadership. Both Héctor and

Isabel are highly respected professionals who were known internationally and respected for their work in education and also in the development of various philanthropic and other organizations that are very action oriented. Their opinions were highly regarded and sought after, and their latest work would be seen as being of great value and might greatly influence existing teachings.

I was eager to hear a little about their work, but a little was not enough. I was not surprised at some of their ideas; in a sense they were reminders of very basic things. However, these very basic things are often forgotten or put aside in politics in our frantic efforts to remain popular and in power. We forget that the basic things hold great power, but we so often conveniently forget them in our search for *greater things* of less importance.

My search for authenticity was challenged by their keen observations and explanations, and this became very significant to me, leaving me to again ponder the validity of my efforts, not only as a person but also as president. It brought to me the old and haunting question of the search for truth, which sometimes plagues us all in any challenge or confusion that causes us to forget our inner voice. It was an extraordinarily challenging time in my presidency, and I was eager to hear what they had to say, particularly about leadership. Many of their explanations and our resulting conversation centred on what they had written about Mexico, although their work applied globally.

Héctor and Isabel told me about many of their ideas and thoughts on how social change might be brought about and included ideas that we often associate only with individuals and groups that are not accepted in the established way of doing things and generally are seen as having little regard for maintaining the status quo. Their ideas strongly stress the importance of individual and collective behavior and focus more on the value of equanimity and justice, as opposed to the protection of the established and legally sanctioned relationship between economic gain and political power. Their work emphasized paying attention to these powers that they saw as arising from the direct or intentional abuse of power, which is aimed not only at maintaining power, but also in propagating the deliberate dismissal of any alternate ideas that might well threaten monopoly of control. It was indicative of the groups who see me and my colleagues as being part of an oligarchy that impeded change and improvement in the lives of Mexicans.

At the time, it seemed to me of some small consequence that Héctor and Isabel acknowledged that, generally, our intentions might well be right, but their contention was that our view of the needs of Mexicans voters is often blurred by our own selfish needs and wants, as well as the undemocratic demands brought about by partisan political action.

At the basis of their work is the belief that although we might well have good intentions, we live in a delusional state, often brought about or reinforced by our socialization and specifically by the values we are taught and practice. This of course is not a new idea, but to hear this with specific recommendations from these respected scholars, to be used as a basis for or focus of any action that would bring about social change, was unusual. They told me that their initial intention was not to focus on individual ethical and moral behavior, but as they continued with their work, they consistently were brought back to the idea that it was time to truly face the crisis of behavior and speak clearly about it with specific recommendations.

At the time I felt somewhat confused and confronted by what they were saying, and that only seemed to threaten the validity and value of my efforts as president and my personal behavior. My questions about their work indicated to them that I initially saw their comments as part of a very strong and pervasive declaration that abruptly ends many serious discussions on things related to the quality of life in Mexico. Mexicans often say something like, "What's the use! In Mexico, everyone and everything is corrupt."This, however, was not at all that they were saying.

Hector read a little from the introduction of their combined work, hoping to clarify and help me to see the wisdom of their comments:

> "Unless we become clearly aware of our delusions, as individuals as well as collectively, we will not be working toward authentic living, nor will we bring about the change needed to stop the damaging path that we are on as human beings. Those who have a leadership role in society have a special responsibility in this respect. We must become teachers, not only in the sense of offering knowledge, but in use and practical application of this in an enabling awareness."

I would later see in their published work an amplification of some of what we discussed at the time, and I quote it here:

"The fundamental human condition is one not only of need, but delusion. The challenges of life bring us great pain and suffering, and without the appropriate enabling structure, both internal and external, that provides us with a healthy opportunity to clearly face and deal with the disagreeable things of life and enable us to develop a realistic view of things, we get caught up in belief systems that have been imposed upon us. This predisposes us to corrupt behavior by limiting our view and our individual search for truth. This resulting behavior does not serve our needs either individually or collectively. It does not lead us to a relatively comfortable and peaceful state in which we are able to grow and continue in a healthy state of development. In spite of the abundance of knowledge in the sciences and humanities, we linger in the knowledge and not the application. We have, in this current era of the history of humanity, become entangled with this knowledge, reinforced in a state of neurotic anxiousness because of the threatening problems that we have created. We have developed an insatiable appetite for knowledge that stays with us and creates a shocking anxious feeling of our inability to respond in a productive way—to do something to alleviate our suffering and halt the destruction of our planet and ourselves along with it.

Our behavior has become self-defeating, both individually and collectively. We are, at this stage, mis-developed and in great need of teachers who will turn this around and lead us to very specific skills and tactics of application of the knowledge, knowledge that is so horribly abused because of its non-application and the mistrust of others. The knowledge that we have in so many fields provides the hope necessary for change, but this positive intellectual assertion must find unity with emotion and feeling to become an active force for change, which is based in recognition of our delusion and in compassion for our sorry state, for ourselves and others. Those who have power to do so must awaken to this and begin to teach ourselves and others how to live. Leaders in society must help people to identify their values and help them see how to live within the social contract and consider commonly accepted ethics that exist. They must stop imposing control and begin to inform and educate and enable individual and collective decision making based on principles of equality."

Their explanations and recommendations clearly focused on personal behavior as the first cause of whatever problems they talked about. They contended that one of the chief problems in the world is that many are caught up in false beliefs in the power and truth of our affiliations. I remembered, as they talked about this, that one of my professors of Political Science had often cited Maimonides and Aristotle's writings on leadership and virtue and particularly repeated these to his students by saying that, "Those who are superior in virtue should receive a greater share in ruling." He saw this as an essential to social development. Héctor and Isabel clearly contended that because of the lack of virtue, political powers often operate within what they considered to be a kind of artificial democracy. It is a kind of democracy that denies full participation of the populace and that is greatly influenced by the function of group affiliation, partisan political action, and ignorance. This is where the importance of their recommendations came to the fore for me.

It is interesting how we filter information and focus on what we have established in our minds and even justify positions on our behavior that we ourselves only tentatively see as the best way of doing things. I remember being taken aback by the contention of what I held as true but dared not articulate: that we operate within a kind of artificial democracy. As they explained this aspect, I clearly filtered out their emphasis on the strong influence of our affiliations on our personal behavior. As they talked about this, I was saying to myself, "Mexicans vote. Our voter turnout is often one of the highest in the world of democracies." I remember strongly reacting to Héctor and Isabel's explanation of various things they were proposing in their writings, but nowhere was my response more filled with questions than in the role of political leadership. It was disappointing to think that *I* might be viewed as a part of a kind of collective tyranny, and I reminded myself that Mexico has one of the best systems and structures in the modern world that allow for democratic action. Our constitution is one of the most comprehensive and democratic documents produced by any country. I remember thinking, *"What bought them to these conclusions?"* Did they think that the attempted ancient Grecian practice of direct democracy was feasible in the current times? I became very curious. Further elaboration of this was part of a dialogue that led well into the night. This brought some greater clarity or perhaps less resistance on my part to accept their need to focus on individual development and behavior and see the direct connection between these things and leadership. I began to find myself in agreement to what they had to say, although the practical application eluded me. It simply seemed very unworkable.

To my surprise, their recommendations did not address any changes in the structure of organizations, either in government or in any other institution in society. When they told me this, I was at last able to hear what they were focusing on, which was education and individual behavior. It is nothing new to say that with the change of individual behavior, collective behavior improves, our organizational structures function better, and our whole society would greatly benefit and become more progressive. However, the great significance of these basic reminders was in the very specific recommendations that accompanied their work. We seldom clearly focus on the dynamics or see that the first cause of any good action that brings about positive change in the quality of life comes from individual behavior. Yes, in politics we are of course concerned about this, and we are ever ready to condemn corruption and vice, particularly within opposing groups, but we usually simply condemn and see the remedies as coming from collective counter-action in our political parties, in lobby groups, and in legislation—when legislation is acted upon with vigilance.

Part of Héctor and Isabel's general recommendations included a very comprehensive national educational plan, which included personal and collective ethics, with specific recommendations for action. In the case of political life, they recommended an interim plan to correct many aspects of political action. They proposed new legislation that would clearly and specifically evaluate and monitor politicians, and anyone holding public office, for their personal behavior. They seemed lost in idealism. However, I was intrigued by their explanations and wondered how and why this very scientifically oriented couple had come to these conclusions. I was eager to hear more.

Héctor and Isabel see the role of leaders in modern society primarily as educators and coordinators, but the leaders of society are unable or unwilling, because of their corrupt behavior, to do this properly, because they often succumb to the circumstance and expectations created by partisan and other groups. It is certainly true that many leaders act like tyrants and sustain their power by corrupt practices. Mexican history has many examples of this. To see changes in this aspect of what they were suggesting was not within my wildest dreams or expectations at the time. Isabel clearly said at one point in our discussion, "Leaders must teach people how to live, but they have to learn how to live themselves." I remember thinking, upon hearing this, that I would be laughed out of the legislature if I were to articulate this in a meeting. I was reacting to what I then thought was a very simplistic answer to all the social problems that we face. I certainly saw their reasoning, particularly in the many explanations of our failure to develop in certain areas and failure to develop new behaviors along with changes in society and modernization meant the loss of informal social contracts as well as the misinterpretation of formal contracts, such as our constitution. They contend that these things, because of the repetition of destructive personal behavior, bring about conflict and confusion and reinforce the focus on maintaining individual vested interests.

"We have also developed a culture of immediacy, and we do not live in the processes of time that are required by any meaningful change," Héctor said. "This in itself—this desire to have things immediately—creates an impediment to living the change in a developmental way and in a process and gives opportunity for the ignorant and the corrupt to impose more control and to advocate for their own selfish needs. People need to be aware of the dynamics of not only personal change, but of collective change and be given the support to bear the difficulties we encounter in the process." These words were very significant to me in the context of Héctor and Isabel's explanations of various parts of their writings and recommendations.

I have always been preoccupied with what I thought was a great burden of constant exploration of how to change things for the better in my life. I had been taught to ask for change—to leave it in the hands of God. When I began not to include God in my planning, I began to ponder precisely what is often referred to as *the dynamics of personal change*. I had never considered the dynamics of personal change, nor did it occur to me that the development of certain tactics in order to do this was even necessary. One just worked for change and improvement by living life and applying what they have learned. Yes, there were certain things one must do to bring about change, but these were external things.

Héctor and Isabel were talking about internal, almost spiritual things. Everything they said was true, but their even mentioning the possibility of the practical application of their recommendations seemed just too idealistic. However, because this message was coming from them, my dear and respected friends, I listened with great interest. Héctor and Isabel's reputation, recognition, and valuable contributions to Mexican society and to the greater academic world command admiration. They enjoy and deserve the attention they receive from anything they teach and write, but I wondered how this new work would be received. In spite of the recognition and admiration, they had recently been very severely attacked in the press and by some of their fellow academics for being too idealistic and in conflict with social and political teachings commonly accepted in educational circles.

In my attempts to clarify my understanding of their recommendations, particularly for political leaders, I asked many questions, including about what they called "the dynamics of personal change." They maintained that this change, this internal dynamic, was the seed, the beginning of the individual and collective change that they were calling for. The explanation seemed very out of the ordinary to me, and I did not really hear it at the time. They told me that they were not talking about anything new here. The significance comes in paying attention to it, thinking of the process as a tactic that brings the attention needed to consciously change our thinking and thus our behavior. They told me that they believe that change or development comes about by the union of the intellect and emotion combined with love and compassion.

"If we pay attention to how we bring about changes in our lives, we will recognize the consistent pattern," Héctor began. He went on to say, "We first intellectually form an idea of what we want, generate an emotional desire for this, and combine this with the knowledge and assertion that we are worthy and deserving of whatever we want. In our society, we have been taught to feel unworthy and undeserving—at the mercy of a benevolent god who had to go to the drastic and unnecessary step of sacrificing himself because of our unworthiness. The love for self and humanity, the practice of compassion and goodwill are part of the education that we need in any plan to bring about social change. This we see as part of what political leaders must learn to do."

It again all sounded a little too sentimental and an over-spiritualization of practical things. Although I understood the sentiment, it remained only sentiment rather than a plan that could be practically applied. I began to wonder if they had had some kind of spiritual experience and had become blinded to certain aspects of the harsh reality of life, particularly the practice of personal values. My understanding, my belief concerning the fundamental human condition prevented even consideration of such idealistic aspirations. I was told almost from the beginning of my cognitive awareness of these things: I was a sinful being, deprived of divine grace, and although my baptism removed the "stain" of original sin, I was forever vulnerable to horrible actions that I must attempt to control. I could only continue to be in alliance with goodness, with God, if I confessed my transgressions and was forgiven by God's representative. I was given very few tactics or practices that would enable me to do this, however.

This choking control by my Catholic teachings still held me in ignorance and with some feeling of being incompetent and unable to arise above the control of the church, a victim of God's representatives, whether or not I was an orthodox believer. I now clearly see that these teachings had left me with the idea that I was operating from these residual vestiges of compelling belief and emotions learned long ago and that these affected my decision making. I was aware of this and had somehow managed to free myself from some of this in my ongoing experiences of life, but I still needed to free myself from the way that I had learned to behave.

My review of this in my mind as I listened to Héctor and Isabel did not bring new light to this, but it did bring me to an awareness of what was their starting point, or "first cause," as they called it. It brought me to my personal behavior and the need to unlearn much of how I operated. I realized too that it was important to reconsider the belief that I had been taught of being at the mercy of the universe and not a partner of it in any way. I perhaps needed to think about what they were saying in a more focused way to make some greater sense of it. There was nothing very profound or extraordinary in what they were saying. The profoundness came in the very idea that this might come about in any society.

What politician is willing to teach people how to live, how to love, how to change their behavior? Was this not the role of clerics and others who specialized in this, or was I thinking in the deluded state, clinging to beliefs that I once claimed to have but never understood? Is our delusion in thinking that we are not affected by once-held beliefs?

Héctor and Isabel clearly see that in Mexico, given its particular history of conflict and social class development, its people are particularly vulnerable and prone to exploitation. Most of the important leadership roles in Mexico are held by people who have had the advantage of wealth and power. Héctor and Isabel are keenly aware of this.

As Héctor talked about his individual development and socialization as a way of giving an example of the development of aspects of his personal behavior, I listened closely. He cited how his socialization had negatively affected his life and the lives of others, including as well all the organized structures within which he lived and worked. His experiences, to a great extent, paralleled my own, and I followed his explanation of his early life with thoughts of my own early beginnings, with thoughts of the parallels in my own life. We both come from very rich and powerful families who have played a major part in the history and development of Mexico. We both lived with great power and the particular isolation that comes with wealth. We also had the privilege of being educated in the best or at least the most expensive schools in Mexico and in the US. We belonged to many groups composed of people with similar values and beliefs. I relied upon this as a basis for my political career. I was president because of this.

As Héctor continued with an explanation of his early socialization, I continued to follow his explanation by thinking of my own early life and development. From childhood, I was taught directly and indirectly by formal teaching and in the behavior modelled by my parents, teachers, and others to accept certain *facts* about various institutions and groups of people. I was taught to judge others by what group they belonged to and to enact upon the generalized information that I had to guide my life and actions. This kind of thinking greatly influenced my decisions in all aspects of my life. Like many others who were socialized in the same way, I tended to make rash generalizations about institutions, groups, and individuals. I too became caught up in *belief* about things that were not necessarily true and in fact were sometimes based in delusion and lies, which are made up for a kind of self-protection and the belief that this was a stable and unchanging part of society and would not change and must be protected.

As a child, I was told how and what to believe. I accepted that this was how things work. However, I never expected to spend the rest of my life struggling with this programming in my individual search for truth. I have always known that we are often programmed, but I never really articulated it in a way that was related to the quality of my personal life, my role in society, or my job as president. I was certainly well aware of this on some level as an individual. I had spent my entire life struggling with this. I could see that Héctor and Isabel had obviously clearly dealt with this question of programming. I had not.

Héctor concluded our discussion by saying that we must of course apply the principle of individualization and that we must take into account the rapidly changing social strata of Mexico. "However," he continued, "we are only different from others who aspire to have the same benefits from society that we do in that we have had an unjust inequitable opportunity to develop because of corrupt personal behavior and because of the protection of wealth and power, the dynamics of which are nowhere more evident than they are in Mexican society."

I was reminded of the haunting faces of poor and victimized Mexicans and the anguish with which I have struggled in this aspect of my presidency. I was reminded of the complexity of life and particularly of equality, this belief that has not been put into practice. I was tired at that point, and I found myself thinking of the effort it took to be idealistic, and I found myself resorting to a kind of lazy refuge in thinking what I had so often criticized: *"What's the use, in Mexico everyone and everything is corrupt. This can't be changed. Doesn't he see this?"*

As I bid Héctor and Isabel goodbye, I knew that much of what they had told me about their work and recommendations would linger in my thoughts, not so much because of my recognition of the validity or even the practicality of what they were saying; these same ideas that were conclusions for them had also been part of my reflections and would continue to be. In addition, much of what they were saying reminded me that I was at a crossroads in my presidency and that I was in need of some kind of a plan as to how I would now face the multitude of problems facing my beloved country. I was particularly concerned with what might be the aftermath of the cancellation of the secret meetings. Although things seemed calm in this regard, I knew that this could not really be the case. I was facing a crisis of what is often called "confidence" in politics, but is more apt to really be an opportunity created by opposition to combat and gain something in a conflict of rivals between two powerful political forces. In this case, much of the loss of confidence was from my own party. The failure of the secret meetings was still very much in my mind.

I had often jokingly said, "Participation in politics creates paranoia, which is proven to be quite real by experience." By calling the suspicion of deliberate action *paranoia*, I was perhaps attempting to mask the reality that politicians do in fact do horrible things to one another and to their constituents in order to get support and votes. We can be very sinister in our pursuit of power.

Public policy is often not a response to the genuine needs of the people. In some cases, people are even manipulated into unwittingly supporting things that do great harm to them. The failure of the extraordinary plans we had made in the secret meetings was an ideal situation to simply gain power or prestige by rallying around those who seemed to be gaining power.

~~~

Later that morning when I was trying to catch up on the loss of sleep, María woke me up to tell me, "Your vice-president wants to speak to you." Doña Margarita would not call unless there was a very serious situation that compelled her to do so.

I would have to return to the capital immediately, ending my escape from the urgency of problems that lay in wait in the background, but set aside in our retreat to the sanctuary of Santa Rosa. My usual official morning telephone briefing came early and shortly after talking to Doña Margarita. It included a reiteration of the recommendation to return to the capital, "As soon as possible."

I sensed that Jorge Maldonado, a senior cabinet member, was a little more reserved in his report, but made it clear that I should return to face what he described as another violent crisis that needed my presence. Violent crises had become almost a routine in Mexico, but some were worse than others. This one apparently needed an "extraordinary response," as Jorge had said. I struggled with some angry feelings of having to leave Santa Rosa sooner than expected, but I knew that I must return.

I was very quickly thrown back into my other world by these two telephone calls, and surprisingly I felt an odd and vague feeling of resentment at the complicated causes of violence in the way that Héctor and Isabel had explained to me. I became angry at this "delusion" that they talked about and particularly the causes of this event that compelled me to return to the capital, even though I did not yet know much about it. It had ended my retreat from the harsh reality, and in a strange way, I knew that this was not really a cause of resentment, but the acceptance of a vague feeling of responsibility and opportunity that had been awakened by the insight that I had gained from my recent encounter with old friends and teachers, hosted by the inspiring atmosphere of our beloved Santa Rosa. I was able to see a seed, however small, that might be a cause for the hope that leads to action and some alleviation of our suffering.

I had my cup of coffee as I waited for the helicopter that would rush me off to the trouble that lay ahead. I truly savour the one cup of coffee that I have each day and usually take time to consciously relax and reflect upon the need to calmly go about what would follow. I was unable to do so on that day.

In the first month of my presidency, I overheard one of my personal guards say to another, "He won't make a good president. He thinks too much." This prediction came to me on that morning. My mind was overwhelmingly flooded with completely opposing views that held the power of a kind of equal conviction. The seed of hope for extraordinary social change brought thoughts of conviction, and the opposition brought thoughts of the need to continue to do what I always have done. I reminded myself, *"For now, get on with the usual job you have to do as president of Mexico!"* The helicopter arrived, and I was taken to the capital—to my other world, and to a briefing of current events that was about to bring a distinct change to everything.

8

MASSACRE AND OUTRAGE

Pain and Suffering

> *Violence is not the problem; it is a consequence of the problem.*
> —Jim Wallis

My brief retreat, or my brief *escape*, as María called it, had provided me with a peaceful and enjoyable time away and a somewhat altered view, or at least various alternate considerations of the issues facing me and the *me* as president. I began to think a lot about the lessons I had learned from this time away; and this somewhat altered view of things became the object of my reflection and planning. It also began to create new insights and a kind of renewed disposition, with courage to face my problems and the problems of Mexico. However, nothing would have given me a sufficiently fortified disposition to keep me from painfully experiencing the violent horror of recent occurrences that had brought me back early from my brief respite. I began to see that there was something very different going on and disturbing in a way in which we could no longer continue to treat what was now happening to our beloved country in the usual way. I again anguished over the loss of the planning in the secret meetings, but my anguish turned to the urgency of the moment and what had just occurred. My thoughts were turned to think of it in another way.

I began to see that what I felt was the depth of the manifestation of an evil energy that we were dealing with. That is to say, I began to think of the totality of the things related to the problems and crisis that faced us and particularly those things related to our so-called drug war in this way. The totality of it was like a massive, growing, uncontained, evil energy. I knew that it would indeed destroy us if we did not face it and change our thoughts about it, our response, and our behavior in relation to it. It was an energy that would destroy me if I did not face it and change my way of thinking about it and my behavior. Perhaps the glimmer of hope, brought about by my recent experiences at Santa Rosa, which I thought had died upon hearing about this latest event, another horrible massacre. However, my hope was still there. It was present in the somewhat vague decision that we must not continue to pretend that the corruption was simply an impediment to our primary actions. However successful we had been with recent reforms and economic development, we could no longer treat these things as the first items on our agenda. Corruption was related to every destructive aspect of life in the Republic. My decision about this was, in a strange way, devoid of anger or revenge, which might have been brought on by the latest developments, although these emotions were present. It was akin to a kind of epiphany—a vague and odd revelation that brought with it a sense of resolution and a strange sense of security. This was also mixed with a sense of regret and guilt for all the inaction related to hiding our fear and greed in activity that had not been sufficient.

I began to think of my plan, a plan apart from anything my government had, but a plan that I was unable to even vaguely articulate in my mind. It was as if I knew that I was hanging on to some kind of an idea of an idealistic and salvific plan in response to the desperate feelings that came with the failure of our policies and efforts to control this corrupt evil. Yet I knew that my thoughts were not futile and that I would continue with the hope that a clear plan would be revealed to me. I would reveal it to myself with continued effort and attention to my continued thoughts, and to the horror of what was happening in our beloved country.

The presenting issue that brought me to the briefing that I received upon my early return from Santa Rosa was not only a painful reminder of what was happening in Mexico; it was also like a horrendous confrontation. The detailed information that was immediately presented was almost unbelievable. I had been told of another massacre, but to hear details of the sinister abduction and murder of an entire cohort of student teachers, along with their professors, a cleric, two nuns, and all of the support staff, along with various others from a state-run school, was particularly painful. Politicians, police, and other government officials were allegedly involved.

We had indeed become numbed to the evils of this war. This incident and the martyrs who had been protesting the corruptness and spread of the evil precisely cited the evil that extended to government officials, the police, and others. This brought me feelings not only of anger, but of great sadness and anguish, but also guilt and a clear sense of embarrassment and shame. As I looked at the photographs of the massacre and the photographs of the victims of this heinous crime, I began to tremble. I felt immense pain from this horror even in my body, and it reinforced a strongly growing resolve to action related to change. The change that I thought must occur was individual personal change. It was the kind of personal change that I had talked about with Héctor and Isabel.

This horrible massacre, in addition to the actions of the evil ones, involved many people who either directly or indirectly represented my government. This was nothing new, but the scale and the blatant and obvious involvement of government officials, police, and members of the armed forces was beyond scandalous. It was beyond talking about impunity or justification. It was like a dark sickness that was attacking innocence in retaliation for its alternate intentions and that had refused to play a part in the corruption of passive silence.

I held the manifestation of my pain in tears until I was well away from others. With the tears came a painful anguish. It was an anguish mixed with the sense of deep despair, anger, and a deep feeling that justice—this most impelling quality that is always our first and last hope—had been violated and that it would bring about an equally powerful retaliation.

The report of this massacre was accompanied by many additional reports showing a dramatic increase in violence and very troubling incidents around the country. The violation of basic civil liberties and the threat to public safety was now much more widespread throughout the Republic. It seemed to be what might be called fully intrinsic. It was a way of life in which we lived and operated. The horrible death toll had reached a staggering number. We truly were in a crisis. It was a crisis that I believed would indeed end in a kind of death if we did not respond to the harsh reality of this threat to our very existence as a nation in control of our affairs.

Following the briefing on this latest massacre and the report of the increased wave of violence and drug-related incidents throughout the Republic, I insisted upon a comprehensive review—"A Review of the State of the Nation," which would not be limited to the war on drugs, but would include a comprehensive assessment of violence and corruption in general. I did not know where this would take us. The fact is, I did not know what else to do or what to call this effort to explore our situation. A *review* was not the correct word. I knew that only a concerted effort would help and that it was somehow related to my somewhat nebulous but compelling thoughts of a new plan of action. We would look at the global situation, looking to the background, as well as the activities and their resulting consequences on every aspect of the functioning of our people and our country.

The war on drugs had been, up to now, essentially a war between the government and the various and rivalling and very powerful drug cartels, which are in conflict and are fighting one another for regional control of their activities. However, this conflict was now extending to target innocent victims both as individuals and groups. It targeted those who did not align themselves in the evil corruption.

The resulting conflict extends to every aspect of life in Mexico. The so-called war is a conflict between the selfish actions of the evil ones and the Mexican people. This is what I wanted to look at. Although it was increasing at that time at an alarming rate, there had not been, in the past, a great use of drugs by Mexicans. This was growing and worrisome. The central activity of the cartels was in transporting drugs from South America to the US and other countries.

My insistence on a comprehensive review of our situation was met with resistance from some members of the cabinet, and this resistance was emphasized in their explanations as to why we should not do this and needed to not do this, because of the negative attention it would bring. I clearly felt the same sinister force from the opposition that came from "trusted colleagues" during and after the last of the secret meetings. Many cabinet members urged me to focus on things that "should be our priority and that were more important to us," meaning that we should continue to act in our usual way. The current valuable corporate investments in our economy from abroad, many seeking to take advantage of cheap wages and exploitive circumstances of production, could also be dealt with at the same time we were doing this review.

However, I insisted upon emphasis and attention on the review and called it a review and planning effort. This brought some surprised looks from some of my cabinet members. This was not unexpected. We had been having planning sessions for the past ten years, reaching back to two former administrations.

"What new insights could we possible come up with?" "We are doing all that we can!" "If we don't talk too much about it, it might just go away." "Look at the futility of the secret meetings." My sarcastic thoughts of what others were supposedly thinking and saying were bothersome to me, but they aided me in dealing with the resistance that I faced in planning this action. I even began to think of the resistance as a kind of fear that comes with an examination of conscience and of the motivating force of regret, a regret of involvement in corruption or from not having done enough to fight against it. I was certainly feeling something of the latter, but knew that we had to pay closer attention and to be more heedful to the causes and remind ourselves of the horrors in order to motivate some greater or different action to combat what we had created, or at least enabled—this evil that surrounded us.

I thought about something that happened to me when I was a teen. I was attending a dance. A fire broke out, and everyone was warned to immediately leave the dance floor and exit the building. Many of us, true to typical teenage behavior, continued to dance, laughing off the very real and present danger that would surely destroy us. With great bravado, we continued to dance and laugh, *bravely* waiting for the last minute to escape the flames, while all around us people were rushing for the exits.

Two of my friends, Jorge Eduardo and Margarita, died dancing. I will never forget their bravado and then their screams as they fell through the floor of flames that suddenly erupted. They descended through the flames into an abyss of horror. It took them from our immediate presence and brought them to us only in fond memory.

~~~

I clearly acknowledged the reasons for the resistance to the review but insisted that it was part of the basic model with which any problem must be faced.

I insisted that we must evaluate, devise, and implement a plan. In this case, it would be a re-evaluation, either because our current evaluation was not valid, our plan was not appropriate, or our implementation was not in alignment with our plan. The articulation of this helped to give some greater meaning for those who did not hold a hidden agenda. We were able to proceed without blatant open conflict.

The policy of my government at that time was not to report or update the public about any drug-related violence and activities beyond what was absolutely necessary. While this was seen as a way of helping to avoid fear and contribute to a sense that things were in control, the real motive was to block information on the extent of the damage and the cost of drug-related activities. We blocked this information as much as we could in order not to attract negative international attention that would compromise investment in the Mexican economy. The official line from the government about the violence and corruption in Mexico was almost ignored. However, the national and international news media covered, if not the details of the cost to the Mexican people, the violence and the horrors of individual occurrences of horrific events, and it was well reported. We knew too that public confidence in our efforts, exacerbated by our suppressive and somewhat deceptive reporting of events, was at an all-time low. It may also have been a manifestation of the growing indifference that many Mexicans felt. Many believed that corruption was a cultural aspect of our country and that no government could really combat this.

The media was ablaze with daily reports of what was happening in the Republic. Many web sites were designed specifically for general reporting, but also for specifics of the war on crime. There was an increase in the reports of the more global aspects of our situation, including the facts and figures of exactly what the cost was to Mexicans and how this prevented the development as well as the supply of desperately needed social services. The exorbitant profits of the drug cartels, who boasted of their riches and decadency, was also being reported in detail, as was the perverse support of their efforts by many Mexicans who profited by their silence and others who profited from their outright support of this corruption. The love of family members who were involved in the evil was also a source of great suffering for many who seemed to be held captive by silence and anguish.

One of the seemingly great paradoxes was in the fact that in spite of the horrors of the occurrences in Mexico, our economy was continuing to do very well and the tourist industry was still booming. The situation held many seemingly great paradoxes and contradictions, but on closer scrutiny, these things were clearly explicable in terms of customary human behavior, including our tendency toward greed, selfishness, and denial. I was beginning to think more and more about personal behavior and what Héctor and Isabel had suggested in our discussion.

My resolve and call to action began in my thoughts. I was not yet secure with these resolutions. It was a kind of *practice* thinking that I often did. "I would no longer succumb to the false praise and the artificial determination to carry on in the pretense that what we were doing was enough, and the right thing for the country. I would no longer tell millions of victimized Mexicans that the measures that my government was taking were adequate and effective in dealing with this extraordinary crisis. I would no longer allow public servants, police, and military personnel to operate with impunity; with the security that they would not be held responsible and accountable. I would no longer attempt to bury the visions of the haunting faces of Mexicans who were at that very moment suffering, not only from the corruption of our actions, but from the deceit that they were not even aware of, including our efforts to shift the focus of responsibility of dealing with many of the violent acts to the individual governors and state administrators of the Republic. I would no longer pretend that many government officials, police, and armed forces were not a part of this evil mess."

What I would do, I did not know, but I started to think of what I would do as "my plan." This plan was without step-by-step ideas or a clear conception of what the proposal was. I only knew that I would not continue to dance while the dance hall was burning down. However, the objective, which was now a clear priority in terms of what my role as president was, dominated my thoughts. The process of what I sometimes see only as my fleeting thoughts was leading me to clearer revelations. I knew too that in addition to what my thoughts were leading me to, my plan was somehow vaguely linked to the experiences of my time at Santa Rosa, what I had been reminded of there, and what I had learned there; and that it would start with the review that I was insisting on.

I also reminded myself that increased awareness of a problem alone is not always enabling. I felt the pressure of this, and I knew that if it is not met with action, it is a useless awareness. Increased awareness can in some cases be overwhelming, and this was one of my concerns in this review if it were not followed by a plan of action.

I was not at that time prepared to openly face any opposition that I knew to be connected with the evil ones; or was this, I wondered, another excuse for inaction? My fears extended to other issues as well. However, I knew that we must begin to think in terms of alternate action and I must convince those in my cabinet whose only impediment to change of policy and action was denial, fear, and a belief that things could not really change in Mexico, to support and to act with me.

Fear was the greatest impediment. The national death toll had reached astounding numbers. Many politicians and government officials and employees had been murdered not only in retaliation for action, but for mere association with opposition to the drug-related activity of the cartels. The fear was very real indeed, but I could not protect anyone from fear, nor did I want to in this instance. Fear, I thought, might be an ally and not an impediment to action.

In spite of many objections, I insisted on the presence of experts from various groups in the country, including human rights groups, educators, psychologists, social workers, sociologists, clerics, and students, members of the opposition party, the press, and a host of others to be involved in our efforts. Many from these groups had been targeted and killed for their opposition to the evil ones. There would be many more observers in our review and planning sessions than there were cabinet members. When someone suggested that it was irregular and perhaps illegal and unconstitutional, I agreed to change this plan. We would continue to meet apart to discuss and plan other pressing matters as a party, and we would call this an extraordinary planning group in aid of government efforts. It would not be a formal cabinet effort. I requested that Doctor Anselmo Gutierrez, a trusted cabinet member, act as coordinator of the group. He accepted immediately, without having to think about it. This immediate decision brought some greater acceptance to what I was insisting upon, as well as giving opportunity to start our sessions immediately.

Anselmo is a laicized priest who has suffered very much from the actions of the evil ones. His son, who was involved in the use and dealing of drugs, was murdered several months ago. His naked and headless body was hung by his outstretched arms from a bridge, along with five others who had dared to be in conflict with a drug cartel they had been working for. Anselmo's wife, who simply could no longer cope with the suffering, died in great anguish shortly after this horrific event. Anselmo, who is a victim-witness to the evil that surrounds us and who is well known for his sense of justice and compassion, was somehow able to carry on in loyal service to the people of Mexico. His coordination of the group would bring much to our efforts.

There was an immediate and overwhelming and enthusiastic and courageous acceptance by many experts and others who wanted to participate in our task. It was a brave act for many who were already threatened for their outspoken views on the cartels. The observers in the group readily accepted the need for confidentiality and our request to, upon completion of the talks, submit a report to my government along with specific recommendations. We would consider these along with the recommendations coming from the cabinet.

In spite of the enthusiasm and courageous acceptance by many invited participants in our extraordinary planning group, some came ambivalently. Cardinal Contreras, who had been a participant in the secret meetings and who had said, "Drastic problems require drastic measures" and "We must proceed" but later seemed to call for no action, only reluctantly came to the meetings. He greeted me at the start of the first session saying, "I'm not sure that this will be productive; we can certainly justifiably confront corruption, but some things simply can be seen and taken into account but must be accepted for what they are." Such ignorance, with aspiration to have ultimate intellectual and moral control, was very disconcerting, and it was a reminder that it perhaps also came with deceit hidden in a false and inapplicable negative platitude, and it was a reminder that there were others like him among the invited participants.

I appointed my dear and trusted friend and senator, Don Alfredo, to act as coordinator of the observers. His enthusiastic response to my request, "Of course, yes, my president," brought me even greater assurance of the need for this task. His love for people and genuine concern for the needs of Mexicans was and is well known, accepted as genuine, and respected by even bitter political enemies. His readily agreed-upon participation brought assurance to some who were ambivalent about the need for this review and what it might bring about and also what it might further reveal about the extent of corruption. Many knew also of his compassion and his readiness to forgive.

The intellectual dishonesty coming from some of the cabinet ministers and a few of the expert observers, as well as the conflict basic to this review, created a somewhat difficult situation in terms of the presentation of the facts, as well as the resulting recommendations. The resistance to face the gravity of the situation with recommendations that would alter our current position, without interfering with individual vested economic and power issues, was very evident in the talks. Our discussions brought me a greater sense of the divide in what I should have counted upon as support and trust. My actions were clearly bringing about some greater clarification of this divide, and I was mindful of the ultimate conflict with those who were directly or indirectly aligned with the evil ones. I realized that this division was part of what we needed to face and see as part of what we were trying to plan. However, this conflict, or the awareness of it, did not hamper the overall impact of the review. The conflict arising from the differences in points of view and values between the cabinet members and the observers seemed to be a catalyst for not only bringing forth factual information, but a great challenge to the intent of the government members. Many seemed primarily focused on changing policy and forceful intervention. It helped us to go beyond this to look at precisely what I was hoping that we would begin to do—to look at the root causes of our dire state.

We did not set a time limit on our meetings. The war on drugs had been going on for many years, but the presenting problem of drug use and distribution and the conflict and destruction that this created lay in our distant past and in our development as a nation. It would be impossible to briefly give even what might be called the *distilled essence* of the various factors involved and the far-reaching influence and consequences of this evil. The presentations and exploration of information for each new topic did, however, bring with it reminders of the reality of the global scope of our problems as well as clear evidence of the root causes of what we were dealing with.

Our comprehensive review started with looking at the source, use, and distribution of drugs, including the international aspects of these issues. This initial exploration lasted for a week—a week of very disturbing reminders of the vastness of the problems and where the responsibilities lie. Often Mexicans look beyond our borders, particularly to Colombia and to the US and often ascribe to them most of the blame for our current state of affairs on the production, transport, and use of drugs. However, an examination of facts regarding the predisposition of our country, in terms of coming to the corrupt state that it was in, was indeed almost like a collective examination of conscience, combined with a social history so riddled with abuse and turmoil, that one of the psychologists who was one of the invited experts said that it was clearly material that indicated therapeutic intervention. In spite of a history of turmoil and abuse, Mexico is also dominated by great and victorious struggles by individuals and groups, which have brought us to be the great nation that we are. We are very proud of our ancient and modern achievements, our racial mix, and our abundantly rich cultural components. We are a patriotic and nationalistic people who take great pride in our particular celebrations of life events and our country's national holidays. We are united in many important things, but we are divided in many ways, which can seem to be paradoxical, but only on the surface.

In spite of our strong sense of nationality, we are a people who very strongly identify with our own state and with our local cultural identities and class. Our divisiveness is also deeply rooted, not only in strong group identification, but also in the divisions that material wealth and the discriminatory use and misuse of power create. We have been subjugated by many nations and struggled under tyrannical control and exploitation. All of these things have contributed to influences that have kept us from developing important levels of equanimity and justice in our public policies. During our meetings, the historical exploration of poverty and our ineffectual education system reminded us of the inequitable divisions and brought our direction to clearly focus on what I saw as our task at hand. It was also a reminder to me that our national policy often failed to take into account the principle of individualization, applying the same tactics in our war on drugs. It was also clear that we are again, as in our historical past, a subjugated people, not by foreign nations, but by the evil ones in our midst.

In the second week of talks, we covered the origin, operation, escalation, propaganda, use of firearms, and human trafficking and smuggling activities of the major cartels. It covered another vast amount of information and clearly showed a recent and very great increase in the activities of the cartels and the perverse behavior of the drug lords, some of whom seem to be almost worshiped, but with great fear of their awful power. The extent of their activities was greatly increasing not only in Mexico, the US, and Colombia, but they also extended to increased activity in lucrative dealings in Central America, parts of Africa, Canada, and parts of Europe. The drug cartels, in spite of being in fierce and very violent and murderous conflict with one another, were not only gaining more and more control of many things in our country, but their evil was also growing internationally.

During the third week of our meetings, we began to look at areas of specific effects of the drug trade on journalism and the media, the massacres and exploitation of Central American migrants, as well as government policy and corruption. These subjects seemed the most troublesome to talk about. We again covered a vast amount of information and somehow languishingly managed to deal with some of the painfully revealing information on government corruption and cover-up. It was revealing primarily in the sense that we were even talking about it and in how the intent of the exploration had indeed some intellectual honesty and was a real attempt to deal with this harsh and confronting reality.

The impact of our review and exploration of the facts was beginning to be clearly evident by the fourth week of the meetings. We were then looking at the casualties we had suffered thus far in our conflict with the drug trade. This, coupled with the effect on human rights and public well-being, brought many emotional and painful reactions. We were all aware of the morality of what was happening in the Republic, and we all had suffered the pain of violence and some sort of casualty from the evil ones. Whether someone was part of the corruption or not, if they lived in Mexico, they had experienced the harmful effects of the drug trade one way or another.

Our discussions were painful and conflictive and seemed to create a disturbing uneasiness. The notion of making recommendations was beginning to be explored by many. The clash of ideas and motives seemed to bring more anger and conflict, and when the discussions and questions came, following presentations of various facts, the divisions became more clearly evident, particularly in the informal contemplation of recommendations, which were not to be part of the content until the end of our discussions. It was evident that the material and the obvious need for action were threatening to those who were, however secretly, opposed to our work.

Anselmo and Alfredo were in constant consultation. Strong in their unity, they stopped the process to give a very strong and clear reiteration of our agreement not to discuss recommendations until we had finished the presentations of the review. In addition, they stressed the need to keep our emotions in check, to endure the difficult process of our review in a way that was a search for the truth and not the usual competitive and destructive manner in which things are solved in conflictive political action. This surprising and very positive confrontation of personal behavior brought silence and obvious regret and perhaps some feelings of guilt to many. This confrontation from two respected members, whose behavior was exemplary, had a great impact. We were able to continue without emotionally laden comments. This, I remember thinking, might well help protect an enabling process in ongoing explorations and planning.

In spite of the talks continuing without the destructive force of the evidence of blatant conflict, this conflict only lay hidden. I had a growing fear of what the recommendations would bring, and I became almost obsessed with the thought that we must somehow clearly address personal behavior in a way that it was not left simply as an implicit factor. I contemplated the fact that part of the solution to corruption was more clearly citing individuals for their wrongdoing and lack of action. Individual behavior caused the problems. I was not personally responsible for the violence that was done outside of the law by the police. I was responsible to deal with it and stop it. It is much more complicated than this, however: ultimately, it is individual behavior that is responsible for the initiation of great corruption and crime, as it is individual behavior that is responsible for the initiation of great good. Individual behavior can bring about dire or desirable consequences.

I remember Héctor and Isabel saying this when we talked about whether or not it was necessary to drastically change the structures of government to bring about needed change. They believed that it was not necessary in Mexico. With the goodwill of individuals, even in error, massive changes can be brought about without changing structures. I was reminded that at the base of their very academic work was a deep concern and love for people. Their efforts in their latest work, as they said, were to look for practical applications for solutions, and this came from awareness, from being mindful of what was really happening. This awareness, brought about by education, can be a very powerful force that can bring about great changes in people's lives.

As we continued with our extraordinary planning meetings, our focus was soon to be turned with full attention to thousands of *manifestations*, as we call them in Mexico, of anger, rebellious rage, and voiced demands from people all over the Republic. We had been alerted by the movement on social media, but we had no idea of the scope and strength of what was happening. It was as if the whole country was exploding in anger, and we were fearful of loss of control that might well escalate to severe dysfunction of government structures and compromise any protection the structures give to public order.

How would we proceed with recommendations, how would we act while surrounded by the thousands of screaming voices, now without hope for justice and peace but calling for our downfall precisely because of our failure to act?

9
THE PLAN

Enabling Structure

...looking after the good and prosperity of the Union.
—Presidential Oath of Office of the United Mexican States

We were in the final week of our meetings, just beginning to talk about our recommendations, when millions of our fellow citizens manifested their anger throughout the Republic. People took to the streets to protest in every city, town, and village in the Republic for several days. The entire country was expressing its outrage. Although the protests were, by Mexican standards, relatively well-organized and peaceful, many of these manifestations did turn into angry mobs, rioting, burning public buildings, and attacking police stations. Protestors in various parts of the Republic carried banners with similarly printed messages. They were angry with the government and blamed me and the entire government for the escalation of the corruption and for operating on a policy of deceit and secrecy. We were also clearly cited for hiding our inaction and the negligence that came from these things—by using violent, brutal force and systematic violation of human rights by the police and the armed forces. The banners also bore brief wordings that labelled the government as useless and despotic. The recent murders of the student teachers and the accompanying protestors had cued these manifestations of anger and mistrust, but the protest was backed and catalyzed by years of a buildup of people living in poverty, suffering, anger, disgust, and the horrible feelings that come with being deceived and exploited. It was very clear how the people of Mexico were, and it could not be denied that many were simply exhausted and demoralized by the continuation of the corruption, yet saw no refuge from those who should be their refuge—my government. This was clear to me. It was very clear to me that this must be addressed.

As I reflected upon the manifestations, some of the photographs of the banners that were used came graphically to my mind: "Kill the President," "Down with the Despots," "Enough Tyranny," "Rise Up and Defeat this Suppressive Regime," and "The Negligent Bastards Must Go." There were none of the usual demands for change or help. The protest was beyond this. It reflected not only anger and despair but also a complete loss of faith in the government. I was reminded of the profound depth of the desperate rage and anger that we were facing.

In spite of my anguish and disgust, mixed with anger and fear, I was somehow able to clearly see that such rage, anger, and destruction held within it a warning. However, it also held an enabling aspect that would help bring about, at least, greater attention and perhaps add to the efforts for real change in the intolerable condition of corruption that we found ourselves in. The public protests were becoming more focused on disappointment with the government than with the corruption of the drug lords. I felt an odd kinship with the protestors that I dared not voice, and I was reminded that in my Oath of Office, I acknowledged that by saying, "…may the Nation demand it of me," it referred to the possibility of my not "looking after the good and prosperity of the Union."

The protest greatly differed in various parts of the Republic. The police and the armed forced also responded in very different ways in various places, but there was no distinctive pattern to the general use of brute force they used against both peaceful and violent protestors. Many people were killed, and many were injured in the protests, including many police officers and many individuals from the armed forces riot squads.

Our usual response to any public outcry and manifestation of this sort was to attempt to assure the people that everything was under control and that the violence and threat of imminent violence was finished. To address the issues the people were protesting would generally be too dangerous, and this was the case in this instance. The anger and disdain for the government would certainly bring more revolt if we attempted to defend our policies and actions at this time. I was clearly reminded in these thoughts that I, as president, was seen by many as being responsible for the personal behavior of all who represented my government.

We continued with many detailed announcements from all over the Republic, informing people of the end and control of the manifestations. It was like a kind of what we call *una pista falsa'*, a "red herring" tactic. It was a way to focus public attention on the resolution of the symptoms, but not the problems. Our continued announcements of resumed calm and order, coupled with an announcement of police reform, seemed so totally inadequate. We dared not *parade* the few leaders of the protests before the press as we usually did with captured cartel chiefs and other criminals of the drug trade. They, unlike the cartel heads and their members, were now the heroes and not the villains. I strongly believed that the extent and the feeling of power that came from the protests would not be held in check for long. Our usual policies, consisting primarily of restraint and control, would not serve for what I wanted for my country. This thought was not new, like so many issues that I had recently dealt with, but it needed clarity in order to enable me to manifest a strong decision regarding my plan—a plan that I knew needed to include, but also to transcend, the recommendations coming from our review meetings.

I knew that the protests would not end. The issues were there lying beneath the surface of a lull in the action of the manifestations in the streets, but they would erupt again and again as an outcry for action. We resumed our talks with this thought and others in my mind. The protests brought about some changes in our meetings. Ambivalence now had no place in our discussions. We continued—some members of the group with a renewed fear of public action, others with the usual bravado and thought of retaliation by punishing those who would dare to confront the government. We now struggled with greater evidence of conflict in the two distinct divisions. Two predominant attitudes remained after the protests. What remained was fear mixed with strong determination by those who had not been tainted by the evil of that we were exploring. The other was a mixture of fear and deeply rooted anger and resentment of our efforts, masked in the collaborative effort of the majority. This fear, anger, and resentment came from those who had somehow been involved in the evil in our midst and who now began to see their own vulnerability.

I wanted so much to deny this division. I yearned to believe that with the outrage now made manifest by so many Mexicans all over the country, we were all united in our efforts and goodwill. We Mexicans have, however, given our long history of struggle with this evil, learned to recognize even subtle vestiges of this powerful and evil opposition and the lack of any sense of goodwill. My thoughts of those among us who falsely smiled in agreement, but who were really against us and who were aligned with the cartels in some way, brought me a mixture of fear and anger. The haunting faces that also again came to me were, however, a catalyst to the growing conviction that what we were doing was related to *my* plan, and that my plan was right. This sustained me, and my mixed feelings of fear and anger were not tainted with the usual feelings of powerlessness.

The high incidence of the contemplation of recommendations throughout our meetings was somewhat encouraged by the agreement we had made at the beginning. We had agreed that the recommendations should be forthcoming in brief and succinct language, as soon as possible, *after* our meetings. This was the case. My government was now ready to consider the recommendations, and we were studying them in contemplation of an urgent cabinet meeting to consider their feasibility and practical application.

The recommendations brought me greater challenge in terms of what the goals of the meetings were or were meant to bring about. Although very concise, they were comprehensive and with little repetition of non-essential explanations. The quickly coming recommendations were clearly divided into "reform with more control" and "control," without too much attention to reform. We continued to meet to discuss our recommendations and would shortly bring them to cabinet. There were some thoughtful and useful ideas, but Mexico needed more than security and reform to combat this nightmare.

As I lay awake nights wondering just what to do about the recommendations—how to deal with them in our upcoming cabinet meeting—I became keenly aware that many of us simply did not know what to do, apart from exerting control, and in our ignorance we form committees to talk endlessly about something that will never be resolved.

Is this what I had done in the formation of the extraordinary planning group in aid of government efforts? No. I knew that it was beneficial and somehow related to the fact that it was not true that we did not know what to do. Many of us *did* in fact know what to do, but we dared not even suggest solutions that were so alien to our way of dealing with things, so radical to our way of thinking, so contrary to our usual political action that we simply fell back on what we had been used to doing in our culture, attempting to control rather than educate, consult, collaborate, and coordinate. Our minds were simply not able to clearly articulate or clearly contemplate what I was beginning to see growing, but not yet clear in my mind, as *my* plan. The recommendations were not an adequate response to the massive problems but were at least of great value in that they brought, along with the recent events of protest, a greater mindfulness to the urgency of an alternate action. I held some hope that together we would acknowledge this and come to some kind of action that would be acceptable to all of the members of my government.

However, my reflections turned from this to what I felt must really be done. It was one of those times that I saw the great value of my thoughts and reflections going all over the place. It was my way of discerning things, and I held this as revelation to myself. I came to some conclusions, and I would follow through, motivated by the need for my own development and the needs of my beloved country.

I would coordinate the meeting slated to explore the recommendations. This was a very valuable exercise. It created a very strong basis of what my plan was, but I *would insist* upon the implementation of my plan and not the usual attempt to simply control subjugated people. However, at that time, I was still not clearly able to even articulate what my plan was, other than somehow to relate to the people of the Republic in a different way: to educate, consult, collaborate, use expert advice, and coordinate, as the basis of what must be done.

A clearer idea of my plan came about. It was developed and supported by my usual mind-wandering reflections and with greater clarity as to what has been revealed to me in terms of how to live, how to act, and how to address the crisis in the Republic. My thoughts brought me not to policies and reform, but back to many important sad and happy memories of my family members and others who have been a part of my life. My prior reflections on life, values, and what I have been struggling with all these years also came to me as reminders of how I had always struggled with how to live and how to act in a way that brings relative peace and some sense of doing the right thing for myself and others.

My recent retreat to our beloved Santa Rosa and my encounters there also prompted much of what came to my mind and what I needed to think about. They were things that also helped bring me to some greater conclusions of what my plan might be. My heavy workload before my retreat had kept me from many encounters with people that I love and respect, and my meetings were strong reminders of very important things in my life that were so influential, so consequential. I now saw that my relationships brought me my truths, my meaning. I knew that in a way that I had not thought of before, that the great and essential meaning in my life and the decisions that I make are intrinsically related to the mindful consideration and love of others, particularly to the people I love and respect. I thought of Padre Toñio, his loving-kindness and compassion, and the face of the stern Romero, turning to joy at his encounter with Padre. I thought of a little girl in Santa Clara de Las Flores, a little girl with a dirty face and tattered clothes who managed to get close to María and tugged at her clothing with her little hand held out for a coin. "Señora, señora," she pleaded. I can still hear her and see her beautiful little face, trying to get María's attention. I remember too how she was sternly led away by one of our security guards. My thoughts also went to Bud and Stella and how they managed, against all odds, to continue to live and give so much in spite of their unspeakable loss. I thought of Guadalupe and her compassion, loyalty, and service. My reflections on my meeting with Héctor and Isabel reminded me of the love they have for people, their dedication to teaching and offering solutions to the problems of our lives. I thought too of the haunting faces of so many Mexicans who, in spite of the suffering they endure, continue with great generosity, love, and compassion, still able to celebrate life in strong family circles and in the many beautiful cultural events of our country. I thought too of the suffering of so many from the misuse of power and ignorance...*the haunting faces.*

In a strange way, I began to better understand and appreciate Alfredo's relationship with the people of Mexico and what motivated him to live such a good life. He loved them; he worried about them and sought to serve them. He valued each encounter with every person he met and took into account what was said to him. He constantly looked at what could be done for them. My thoughts led me to how the lives, how the love for and inspiration of others help shape our values and actions. Our own personally revealed truths find a supportive alliance in the truths of others, and we are encouraged by this in our desire to do what is right. The beliefs and values that had been assigned to me in my early formation simply served only for *consideration*. I did not see them as a guide to my life. Many of these beliefs had been revealed to me as mine within my own reckoning, but after considerable thoughtful effort and critical thinking, many were revealed as hollow, useless things like useless platitudes and slogans that did not serve me now in the decisions that I must make. I must continue to fight the arrogance that is deeply rooted in having been born in privilege. I would implement my plan only with the revealed truths that I had selectively practiced for myself, my family members, close friends, and individuals for which I had esteem. I would try to relate to the people of Mexico with loving-kindness and compassion, with understanding and truth. As president, this would mean coordinating their aspirations for happiness in a new way, educating, encouraging, and advocating within the organizational structures to respond to their needs. I would also cite the failures of individuals who did not do or were not capable of doing their duty and who disallowed self-determination for those who were striving for a new life, free from corruption. I would deal with the people of Mexico with humility, and I would act against the domineering and arrogant attitudes of other *servants* of the people in my government. The practical application, in terms of the content of this effort, was, however, still somewhat elusive.

What I now see as a strength, in addition to thoughts that come with such profound meaning and result in important decisions, I often have counter thoughts and hold these in a seemingly contradictory way and with equal conviction. This often results in inaction if I see this dynamic as a manifestation of insecurity. However, in this case, the only thoughts that counteracted my decision to implement my plan confronted me with, *"How would I relate this to the people of Mexico—what words would I use?"* Clearly not the same jargon, platitudes, and promises that helped bring me to the presidency and that I repeated in my acceptance speech. However, therein was the answer to the practical application of my plan. I would begin to talk to the people. I would use new words. I would talk to them as their president, but I would talk to them in the same way that I would talk to anyone who I loved and who I wanted to help.

I would start by talking to the people of the Republic, to my people, to the people I love and respect and want to serve. I would start to talk to them about what would unite us in the challenges that we face, the unprecedented challenges that bring about the circumstances that seem to deny us our rights and opportunity, and the functioning of the existing and potentially enabling structures that are in place in our country. I would talk to them about what denies us the opportunities that support and allow our growth and development in our pursuit of happiness and peace.

My words would be an attempt to say what has been developing within me ever since I became president, stretching back to my first memories. I would acknowledge that what I was doing was really a part of a greater movement brought about by many things, including the protest and confrontation in which the people of Mexico were manifesting their loss of trust in my leadership and in the government.

With these thoughts, my mind went back to the meetings and our recommendations. We would bring these to our cabinet meeting the following week and attempt to revise our policies and actions. We would again return to the same process with the same options that brought us to where we were. The recommendations would only bring us back to either more force, or force with reform. We needed to see the reality that these things were simply not working.

I wondered what the reaction to my plan would be. I wondered how to present this in a way that recognized the value of the process that we had just completed. As I thought about this and the potential conflict and disagreement when I presented my plan to cabinet, it became clear to me that the priority was not there. I knew that I could not incorporate what I wanted to do, in spite of its importance, in the exploration of recommendations that centred on control and reform. It became clearer to me, contemplating details of what I would do.

I would begin to speak to the people of Mexico in the new way that I had in my plan, by acknowledging the harsh reality of corruption and its great threat to our country. I would share with them the results of our recent extraordinary meetings and continue to engage with them by enabling them to be involved in any collective action administered by our organizations in our great and common task, clearly facing the disagreeable things of life and dealing with them in a way that would lead to the improvement and changes that we wanted. I would do this by directly speaking to the people of Mexico in weekly television and radio programs, incorporating the things that have been revealed to me about leadership. I would engage the rich resources of educators and others to help in this task. I would start with this practical application of my plan and be open to what was to become my new role as a leader and begin to practice what I now saw was my authentic mandate.

~~~

The decision to bring my plan to the next cabinet meeting came with thoughts laden with ambivalence—ambivalence, my old enemy, but at times my old friend—to wait or to act now, sometimes with confidence, at other times without. This ambivalence triggered thoughts of many of the events that have led to numerous actions in my presidency, particularly those that were in conflict with others, mainly with members of my cabinet.

My thoughts about the origin of this conflict brought me to a conversation that I had had with María. She had posed the question: "Do you think that perhaps you have gone too far in some of your efforts...that you have gone beyond what is expected of a president and as a leader of your party?" Definition and practice of one's role in Mexican society, particularly in politics where control and power often define what is expected, are always important concerns.

Many of the proposals that I had recently been bringing to my cabinet for consideration were clearly things that anyone with even a superficial knowledge of the needs of Mexicans would see as desirable and beneficial and should have been easily agreed to. However, conflict ensued in spite of these things. I began to see that this conflict came because I was perceived as not working within my expected role. I was reminded of María's keen observation and teaching skills. She was right. My *threatening* actions and proposals, however, needed to continue, but with a clearer mindfulness of the potential conflict they held. My clearer realization of this somehow halted my ambivalence about bringing the announcement of my plan to cabinet. I would bring it but hope for the right moment to do so.

I wondered too if my view and actions might well be perceived as working to change the role of government, if not the role of the president. Was this also true in the greater context, in the context of those who had control and power beyond politics? I remember the words of Cardinal Contreras, in response to a suggestion that I pondered in a conversation that we had about things that touched on the spiritual life of poor Mexicans. Upon hearing my suggestion, which included some political action, he repeated several times,

"That is not your role, Miguel…that is not your job! You are not a cleric, Miguel. You are a politician!" I remember being somewhat shocked by his comments and thinking how superficial and ridiculous they were.

The history and development of politics in Mexico has a consistency regarding decision-making. Regardless of which politician made or described which decision or the manner in which decisions were made and carried out or the process itself, the focus has always been on control, authority, and maintaining order. These have been the characteristics that have been constantly emphasized. Some of the many and diverse responsibilities of government have been almost ignored or given very low priority because of the conflictual nature of our history. Government in Mexico has tended to take a defensive role because of this conflict and because of the pervasive and ongoing general opposition to various governments. The response to the needs of the more powerless citizens has been a low priority. Keeping order and fixing legal relations, the regulation of trade and industry, and the regulation of legal relations, labour contracts, and property rights has taken precedence over such things as the care of natural resources, education, and the care of the poor, aged, and infirm, issues that were left to others, primarily to the church.

Any change of focus brings conflict and confusion. I contemplated the practical application of my plan and the conflict that would come—not only from the evil corrupt ones in or associated with the drug trade, but from legally vested interests whose loyalties lay in maintaining the status quo and their own interests—greedy interests that lie far from equanimity and justice and that bordered on and in many cases were supported by corruption.

The primary goal of my plan was to educate. To teach individuals and groups how to protect, maintain, and to improve the quality of their lives by fully taking advantage of and using the provisions under our constitution. Our constitution very clearly states and defines the rights and freedoms of all Mexicans. It also very clearly states and defines the responsibilities of all Mexicans and the government. The issue of the right to services that are currently greatly compromised by indifference and corruption within the existing governmental institutions would be addressed. The various presentations would not only provide information on how to access and advocate for appropriate services and the amplification of services within the existing governmental structures, but would include a consultative and collaborative aspect, inviting input, suggestions, and a means for advocacy, for problem solving.

This educative aspect would also be addressed to the many government employees and officials in their service to their fellow citizens. Government officials and employees, whether because of indifference, lack of expectations, or corruption, often fail in what I consider to be an intrinsic part of their work as public servants. They fail to practice what I call their *dual role*. They fail to advocate for people within the organizational structures for services that are lacking.

My mind goes back to many years ago when I was a manager of a particular governmental social service agency. A group of managers were being advised by a regional manager on how to deal with demanding clients. The content presented to us was not only recommending that we use undue control and intimidation, it recommended abusive behavior. Our corrupt complacency was obvious in our failure to complain on behalf of and advocate for our clients. We jokingly talked about our consistent complacency and failure to speak up as "Dealing with it in the hallways" as we exited meetings. Many government employees talk about abuses and failure of government services *in the hallways*, succumbing to intimidation and corruption and not being a part of the development of equanimity and justice.

With advice and information from many expert speakers, Mexicans will be given, with respect, encouragement, and kindness, the opportunity to more fully and appropriately participate in the aspects of government that exist to help them to live in harmony and peace. The information in the lectures and the topics of various courses, will, largely depend upon the input, criticism, and issues presented in the consultation that will be a part of each presentation. However, the plan is to include a comprehensive list of topics, all related to total personal wellness, and achieve this under the provisions of our constitution and institutions. While the teaching of assertiveness without aggression will be a central educative aspect, teaching and consultation on such topics as life purpose, values, dealing with corruption, and family life are also part of the plan.

~~~

With the beginning efforts of cabinet to consider the final

recommendations coming from our meetings, it became evident that the deep divisions were not only based on the differences between "control of people" and "control of people with reform." The control that was more evident in our meetings centred upon delaying any decision making, as opposed to moving forward. The discussions would not be completed quickly, and this was clearly acknowledged.

Amidst discussions of the recommendations, I introduced my decision, as an interim plan, to directly speak to the Mexican people and continue with weekly television and radio programs, starting with reviewing the findings in our meetings and proceeding with the planned educative and consultative talks. I was so surprised at the general acceptance of what I was telling my cabinet that it brought me a very uneasy feeling. Although it was met with some objection and ambivalence, the plan was generally supported; perhaps I only saw the significance of what this might lead to! Nevertheless, I was very surprised and grateful for the support, even if it was support only in indifference. I also suspected that some saw it as a positive move and a preparation for the eventual presentation of our recommendations. However, many others saw this as supporting their delay tactics. I knew too that I could not turn back. The practical plan of implementation brought with it a very firm assurance that what I was doing must be done for myself and for Mexico.

In spite of the general acceptance of my plan, perhaps because of the usual operation of political maneuverings and the relatively easy acceptance by cabinet of my plan, I had, a strange feeling related to the deep division that I felt with other politicians over certain issues, that I was somehow secretly manipulating them. I felt a strange insecurity related to my new *secret* plan—secret not because I was holding back information, but in the fact that they did not see the significance of what I was about to do. We all have what might well be called *hidden agendas* in every relationship. It seems fundamental that we all explore things wanting to come to some sense of unity, but always looking to find acceptance by others of our own tentative truths and to relate to others in a dialogue on this basis.

I left these feelings, but they brought me other thoughts that lay at the background of what I was doing; more important and authentic alliances with others who would understand what I was doing.

I had not talked to anyone in detail about the subject matter of the talks that I would give except with María and Doña Margarita. In a strange way, I had held off doing this because the advice and warnings that I feared would be forthcoming might well create just enough ambivalence to keep me from acting with confidence. I was somewhat fearful of the very things that were enabling to me, the support and love of friends and trusted colleagues, and I knew too that this false fear was perhaps partially a creation of my own insecurities, but much more due to the corrupted environment within this era of evil influence in our country and the fact that political power was not aloof from this influence that held power over our every action.

It was not difficult to decide whom to consult about my plan. I had always talked about the important things with these people. María and I met with my brother Diego and Marta Ana, my dear friend and advisor Don Alfredo, Don Alberto Rodriguez Robles, Alfonso Mario Xaxalpa, Bud and Stella, Héctor and Isabel, Anselmo, and of course Doña Margarita. I contacted all of them and told them that I needed to talk about an important issue and wanted their feedback and recommendations. I was grateful that they all immediately responded to my unusual request. Doña Margarita made all the arrangements for a weekend-long meeting at Santa Rosa.

Meeting and discussing my plan with my most trusted and beloved friends was very powerful and sustaining. It was powerful in the sense that it was comfortable and assuring to be in the company of trusted people who were not at odds with me or with one another. It was a meeting free from the evil influence of petty partisan competition to which I was so accustomed. It was not only sustaining but also truly enabling in the confidence, trust, and wise advice that was freely given to me, void of the influence of the pressures of corruption.

I was glad for the opportunity to discuss my plan and the many implications of what I was about to do, but I also was reminded that this was not my plan alone; it was something that was happening far beyond the borders of my own thoughts and personal transformation. This became clear to me in the exploration with the others. In my concerns at beginning to practically apply my plan, I was clearly reminded that the process had implications far beyond what I was contemplating in the reaction of fellow politicians and the Mexican public.

As part of our discussions, which ranged from global to local aspects of the challenges facing our world and our country, Héctor and Isabel commented on what I was about to do. What they said remained in my mind as a kind of summary, not only of my plan but what was happening in the greater context of the global community. This reiteration was restructured to include a greater view, which we all enthusiastically recognized. It was precisely what their latest writing was about. Their work was finished and was about to be published.

Héctor and Isabel, referring back to our long discussion that we had had at Santa Rosa when I was on my great escape from the failure of *the Secret Plan*, did not remind me that I was about to take a great risk; they knew that I accepted this. They did, however, tell us that what I was about to do was the beginning step in what they referred to as "a long and arduous struggle."

Héctor and Isabel requested that I reiterate concisely what it was that inspired me to act to change things and what exactly was I proposing and that I should do this in relation to global implications, not just in terms of what was happening in Mexico. They are wise educators. I saw the wisdom of this and in their suggestion that we meet shortly after my initial speech. This meeting would provide a valuable review as well as planning for what presentations would follow my speech.

Everyone involved committed to continuing with me as team and helping me to implement my plan. They and others would help me not only to prioritize the various things that María, Doña Margarita, and I had been working on, but also to review and suggest content and speakers and so on. I was delighted and grateful for their generous support.

I was warned of the possible and painful and destructive responses; ones that I was already aware of. However, there was no need to defend and explain the "what and why" of my plan. Although somewhat surprisingly—yet some ambivalence, only because of fear of my being hurt in some way—there was complete support for and accord in what I was doing. This was what I wanted and needed at this time. It was new to me not feel a false guilt and weakness for asking for this help and rediscovering what had been put aside, the need for the care of and interaction with people one loves and trusts. Instead of the accustomed distrust and seeing consultation as a weakness, my friends applauded the strength of consultation and the opportunity to give advice and support to what they all saw as part of their right and responsibility *as* my friends. They also saw this as part of their civic responsibility as Mexicans living in the midst of the evil influence that surrounded us at that time.

Héctor and Isabel were glad to be a part of the ongoing planning for the presentations, and I invited them to be the first guests in the broadcasts to speak to their fellow Mexicans. They quickly agreed.

The others followed Héctor and Isabel and recommended other people from all walks of life in our country—people who would speak with great understanding and knowledge, but with frankness and encouragement—people who knew and were very conscious of the great need we had at this time in our history. The recommendations clearly indicated a sense of understanding of and unity in what I was trying to do, and I was glad that we had time for the opportunity to read a draft of my speech for the first broadcast, to which I later added many of the recommendations that were forthcoming.

Our weekend ended with a great feeling of strength and resolve. Every member of this very supportive alliance would continue to meet with me as a team and be a part of the presentations to the people of Mexico that were to follow my first speech. We agreed to continue to meet in support—not only of what I was attempting to do, but also in support of one another in a clear commitment. I saw this as a great alliance of risk, but also of a great sense of purpose, filled with the kind of meaning that gives strength to our pursuit of the meaning of life and our service to others.

I felt a great deal of gratitude and unity with these people. So many of my contacts and advisors are ready only to give words. María, Diego, Marta Ana, Alfredo, Alfonso, Bud, Stella, Héctor, Isabel, Anselmo, and Doña Margarita were risking their very lives in the practical application of their efforts, efforts that would be very visible in what we were doing, visible to those who might well seek to destroy them in their tyrannical evil pursuits. The fear for my life and the lives of others in retaliation, even for alliance, was very present to me at this time.

10
MY SPEECH TO THE NATION

The Practical Application of Hope

*My task, which I am trying to achieve is, by the power of the written word,
to make you hear, to make you feel. It is, before all, to make you see.*
—Joseph Conrad, *Lord Jim*

My speech was televised and broadcast by all networks in the republic. It was published the same day in *Diario Oficial de la Federación*, Official Journal of the Federation:

> When I was elected to be your president, I was very eager to tell you many things in my acceptance speech and to tell you how grateful and pleased I was to be your president. In that speech, I initially spoke to you of what was in the minds of all of us at that time—the need for change in Mexico. We were a country in need of change that would remove us from being the victims of violence and corruption—this violence and corruption that had become so intrinsically a part of our lives, the scope of which has extended beyond what might be called normal for any society. This evil had become a sociological phenomenon and a great challenge to us all. I spoke to you of my acceptance and determination to deal with the difficult situation and the dire problems that faced me, that faced all of us. I told you that I would honour your trust and that I would keep my promise to uphold democracy and work toward changing things for all Mexicans.

I spoke to you of unity, of national reconciliation and full democratic participation. I told you that I understand the changes needed in order to address the new reality that we find ourselves in, in the modern world, and of the need for the full freedoms of democracy and social participation. I spoke to you of the need for a modern presidency—honest, responsible, respectful, democratic, transparent, open to criticism, and willing to listen and take into account the voices of all Mexicans—and my desire to lead you in attaining your aspirations for the improvement of the quality of your lives. I promised you these things.

I told you that I looked forward to helping make Mexico a modern and successful country that recognizes the potential and the talent of every citizen. I cited the needs of the large population of our youth and the difficulties they face in getting an education and finding jobs.

I spoke to you of a Mexico that cannot be held inactive by the past and that a democratic government is a government that respects, enforces, and preserves the law. I spoke of the continuation of the fight against crime with a new strategy to reduce the violence that threatened the very lives of us all. I reminded you that there would be no agreement, no contract with organized crime, and that there would be no truce in our mission against this corruption.

I also spoke of important unity with the governors and the mayor of the city of Mexico and how this working together was also a vital thing for all our institutions and organizations in Mexico and how I would work with all powers and levels of government to initiate new understandings, agreements, and goals. I promised open dialogue with parliamentary leadership in order to introduce and bring about reforms for various things that would improve the quality of life for Mexicans.

We have great poverty and inequality in our country. I told you of my concern and commitment to change this and to turn things around for so many who are without hope for a brighter future.

I also spoke to you about our love for our country and of the many things that we clearly hold dear, enjoy, and have struggled to achieve in the long history of our development. I told you all these things and more. I met with the outgoing president and his team for an orderly and transparent transition and subsequently began my journey with you as your president. I began this journey as many have done before, with great enthusiasm, pride, and intent to follow through with all the things I told you that I would do.

My words to you then and in subsequent speeches, both formal and informal, often contained a reiteration of these things, which formed, in a sense, my contract with you—my promise to you. In the oath of office that every president of the Republic recites, I stated:

> "I affirm to follow and uphold the political constitution of the United Mexican States and the laws that emanate from it and to perform the office of president of the Republic that the people have conferred upon me with loyalty and patriotism, in all actions looking after the good and prosperity of the Union; and if I do not fulfill these obligations, may the Nation demand it of me."

In my efforts as a Mexican and as your president, I continually reflect upon the words that I spoke to you in my acceptance speech and in the oath of office. In Mexico today, we need to clearly evaluate our situation and remind ourselves of our values and our commitment to one another. The constant examination of governmental workings and efforts, which is a part of public office and my part in these things, has brought me to what I want to say to you now. All of the words in my acceptance speech and in the oath of office are words that all politicians use and continue to repeat—motivating, promising, and informing people. They are good words and good promises, and those who use these words usually intend them as promises arising from a great sense of responsibility and motivation to serve. Today, however, I want to speak to you in a new way. I want to speak to you with greater frankness, asking for your attention and careful consideration of what I am about to tell you.

We do not need to be reminded that we live in a country of great wealth—in our people and resources, the great natural beauty in every part of our nation, and the great strength in the values and customs that we have developed. We are having success in our development of industry and economically. We are recognized with great admiration internationally and enjoy the benefits that come with so many foreign residents and visitors who come to us. We have also lived through great turmoil and violence, yet we have not succumbed to accepting failure. We continue to celebrate life in our families and communities, in our temples, in our organizations, and in the wonderful and extraordinary way Mexicans have of relating one to another, in friendliness and with feelings of solidarity, brought about by our history and sustained by our rich cultural values.

We are a great nation of enormous beauty and strength. We are like a beautiful piñata, bearing wonderful things to help us enjoy and celebrate life. These things are true. However, to be reminded of the wonderful things of our country and not to look at the horrible suffering and anguish of those who do not share in these things, in the abundance of material things that we have, would be a great injustice, just as is the very existence of the great poverty itself.

Many of you who are watching and listening to these words live in deep poverty amidst the great wealth of our country, yet you continue to rejoice with those who have more, patiently looking for justice and hoping to be treated with respect and justice. However, prosperity is only a dream for you—for many Mexicans. Some progress has been made, but the great social and economic gap is often not seen or is ignored by many in the belief that economic prosperity will trickle down to the poor. However, it fails to, because of greed and corruption—this intrinsic corruption that keeps all of us from functioning to serve your needs instead of combating the evil in our midst. Billions of pesos are spent in combat of this evil instead of in developmental services that would help rid our country of this dire poverty. There are of course many factors involved in this great problem, but at the base of this is corrupt personal behavior. These behaviors prevent the workings of all our institutions—private and governmental—that seek to attain some greater material equanimity and justice. This is our great failure.

My dear friends and fellow Mexicans, we are fast becoming like an empty piñata. We are being destroyed by an evil among us that we must combat in a new way. I can repeat to you what you have heard many times about what your government is doing to serve you in our efforts to develop economically and socially and in our efforts to combat violence and corruption. You will hear these things again, but not today. Today I want to speak to you, as I said, in a new way. I will not tell you anything new. I will remind you of many things that we need reminders of, and with these reminders comes an appeal to do something that we are not always willing to do and that we are not sometimes skilled at—to work together and to combat the evil in our midst that is destroying us. This is an appeal, first, to listen and then consider how we can change things together. Your government is not a saviour, nor is it your boss. We all must do this.

At the basis of the crisis of corruption in Mexico is the issue of individual personal behavior. We are not alone in the individual acts of goodness or evil that we do. We affect one another. My future is in your hands, and yours is in mine. We can see this so clearly in Mexico in the evil that is spreading and growing in strength among us. Many of us have become desensitized to the corruption. Many are so overwhelmed by it that they themselves have become corrupt and violent. We see this corruption all around us. We see it even in actions of individuals who attempt to hide in the protection of organizations that exist to govern, educate, defend, organize, protect, and serve us in various ways. Our corrupt behavior is reflected in the collective action of structures that are no longer able to adequately serve to enable an honourable, safe, productive, and happy lifestyle for all Mexicans. These things have led us to a situation where, as a whole, we are in great conflict with ourselves. We are at war with ourselves. In addition, we are beginning to lose the ability to work together in unity when we are faced with crisis. This loss brings a dreadful fear. We must not lose this strength of unity that comes during crisis. We know that in our families, however deeply we may be divided in certain issues, in conflictive threats from without, we come together and support one another. We must not lose the strength of this action as a nation. It is vital to our existence. We need to tap our strengths as never before and have action plans that transcend simple control of the problems that threaten us all.

Mexico has one of the most comprehensive constitutions in the world. It is an agreement. It is a contract. It is a pact between the government and the people, indicating rights and responsibilities. It does not merely sanction economic relationships between government and capitalist enterprise. This noble document was the first constitution in the world that set out social rights of all citizens. Mexico has the organizational structures in place to serve and protect the needs of its citizens. We have the economic success that will help us to implement reform and initiate programs that will eradicate dire poverty. All of these things are working strongly to enable us to continue with the aspirations and actions implicit in our great revolution, but now, more than ever before in our history, we need to remind ourselves how to do this, how to prevent the corruption among us and in our organizations from ruining our great nation—from ruining our lives. Much of what we are doing is preventing us from wisely using our organizations and leading us to a kind of despair in terms of recovering from the corruption we are beginning to live with in relative resignation. This conflict with ourselves can only be resolved by, yes, solidarity and unity, but more by changing our behavior, changing our actions.

I want to respond to what many have said in recent and past protests and manifestations. You have told my government and me that we are not doing our job. I want to listen to this because I know that we need to change what we are doing in order to honour our pledge to you. I want also to honour the promise that I have made to you, not only out of a sense of obligation by oath, but because I love you and want the best for you. I want to be with you, to improve, and to enjoy all the benefits that come with being a Mexican. In a review of my role, of my behavior, I see that I must continue to be focused on control and protection and do all the things that I have been doing, but now I must put more effort into enabling and honouring your strength and reminding you of what we must do together. I am in no way negating the first responsibility of the government, which is to protect. I am saying that a government that has so much opposition in the form of corruption, either from within or externally, either by intent or by circumstance, cannot function and fulfill its role. A contract implies two sides. Your government, I repeat, is not a saviour; it is an enabling structure that works with you to serve the valid needs and wants of every Mexican. We can only be productive with mutual cooperation and actions that stem from the love we have for one another, for our country, and for our way of life.

In one aspect of my role as president, I act as an enabler, as one who empowers. In this particular role and with a plan that I have, I want to act as a coordinator, an educator, and an enabler. I want to act with you to inform, evaluate, and not only tell you what our government is doing, but to consult and plan with you and make these plans a part of our action. This will include ongoing evaluation in our efforts to remind ourselves of our greatness and our great capacity to change and to conquer in this war against corruption in our midst. Mindful of the great suffering of many of our brothers and sisters because of the evil we are combating, this will lead us to a more authentic and honest development and sharing of our resources and to a renewed sense of worth and service to ourselves—to one another. For many, this is but a reminder of what you are already doing, and I salute your efforts that are sometimes not well acknowledged. For some, it will be a reminder of what we can do, and for some, it will be a confrontation and a demand to radically change your behavior. For all of us, I hope that it is an opportunity to work together to act in this crisis in order to move forward with hope and renewed power to make Mexico a better place, a more just place, for one another, for our spouses, our children, our grandchildren—for all Mexicans.

I will be talking to you every week in an hourly program to be broadcast to the entire nation, about my plan and about our mutual efforts. We have in Mexico some of the greatest educators and thinkers in the world. Some have very important recommendations to make that will help. They can help us. Some of them will be invited to talk to us and help us in our task. In addition to the various invited educators, as well as others who can help us in our efforts, we will invite the heads of our states, cities, towns, and villages to be a part of what we are doing and to offer their support, informing us of what they are doing as your representatives to protect and serve your needs.

Awareness is one of the basic intentions of my plan with you. However, we know that awareness alone is seldom enabling. It must be accompanied by motivation, opportunity, and action. This is the intent of my plan to explore things with you. We all have a role to play in the development of our country. Our individual roles as fathers and mothers, as children, as siblings, as workers, as servants, as merchants, as educators, as politicians, as professionals, as clerics, or whatever our roles are—they are accompanied by a role that we often are prevented from practicing. Our dual role includes not only confronting the blatant corrupt personal behavior of others, but also condemning it and insisting on change. This action will impact and change behavior within the organizational structures in order that they be more responsive to all our needs. Mexicans, at times, do not work well together. We must consider this and change this. We must change our personal behavior and encourage one another to do so. I know, as I say this to you, that this will be one of the hardest things to understand, and with the help of others, I will expand on this issue later, but I wanted to be frank with you and have you start thinking about this.

Mexico has in place organizations and structures that can well serve our needs, as well as laws that protect our liberties and welfare. I will not tell you that I currently propose new laws that will rescue us by additional structures. If these organizations are working well and are without corruption, they will lead to the reforms we need. What we need now is for these organizations and structures to function with transparency and honesty in order to serve our needs and continue to develop new policies and actions. I see this as being a very important thing. This in itself will bring about great change and renewed confidence in our structures and organizations.

At this time of great need, however, I am proposing extraordinary legislation that would combat corruption at its source—individual personal behavior. This legislation would provide for independent monitoring of personal behavior in all our institutions and government structures. This will require the establishment of a new organization that will act throughout the country. While we must continue to protect individual expression and rights, any illegal behavior that is seen as impeding service to us in an act of deception and misuse of trust and authority in any of these organizations will be brought before the courts. In the current context in our country, certain acts that impede our development so seriously affect our journey to wellbeing that they can well be seen as illegal acts of treason. I frankly state this as a fact that will be dealt with and not as a threat. We of course have legislation that covers this. My intent is to bring this to a clearer focus as a means of greater vigilance and control. I also see the need for an educative aspect in order to combat the phenomenon that is happening within the growing corrupt atmosphere that threatens to become the norm. I will be talking about this in the upcoming weeks.

Your government is in the final stages of a lengthy and comprehensive exploration of the causes and results of the problems facing our country. We have been meeting with various experts and others in an extraordinary planning group in aid of government efforts, exploring and evaluating our pressing problems in Mexico. We are now formulating recommendations that we hope to implement as soon as possible. This exploration and planning partially helped me to formulate the initiative that I am telling you about today and what I am beginning with you in my weekly meetings via the media.

My plan also came about through the failure of what is now known as "the secret meetings." The exploration and planning in these meetings seemed to be a total failure. This failure, however, brought great success in the establishment of my thoughts and plans of what I must now do as your president. I will also be talking to you about this later. For now, I want to say to you that in our next meeting, I will, with the help of others, be informing you of everything that we have done in the extraordinary planning group in aid of government efforts. The information, as painful as it is to be reminded of, as well as the implicit implications for action by government and all Mexicans, I hope, will be of great value to you in your daily activities made difficult by the corruption and violence that surrounds us—that extends even to our families and friends. I hope that it will form a basis of what will follow in my presentations to you. It helped to form part of the basis of what I now want to tell you.

The extraordinary planning group was composed of many experts and others who are not a part of government, as well as by representatives of our opposition party. The facts of what were presented to us were, for some, reminders of what we already know. For others it was a startling discovery, and for others an embarrassment because of what they are involved in. We, the government, reviewed these with others, in an attempt to gain new insights and recommendations by which to continue our efforts, both immediate and long term, in our service to you. We particularly examined how this is related to corruption and violence resulting from the drug trade.

The review was comprehensive, but I now, with great frankness and with great sadness, tell you that the extent of government corruption and violence was greatly beyond what we thought it was. I also want to say to you that I am not individually personally responsible for the escalation of the corruption and for operating on a policy of deceit and secrecy, nor is it the official policy of your government. However, we are, in many ways, a definite part of the problem in the same way that all Mexicans are. We must face this. We must acknowledge this together. Individual personal behavior is at the root of corruption and violence and the resulting grave problems in our country. The grave problems that we are facing now, which affect all of us, and the quality of our lives and the lives of our children and grandchildren, are the result of ill will—of deliberate personal evil action, which is done with disregard for the consequences for self or others. The behavior that supports this evil, that enables it to exist to the extent that it currently does, is often done in ignorance, fear, and without seeing any alternative. Many of us are accommodating this evil. We are often victims of the evil without much awareness as to what extent. The horrors of recent events have again reminded many of us of this and brought us to a new and painful awareness that seems to come with greater force with each violent incident.

This brings me to say that what I am proposing in ongoing presentations will, in all likelihood, bring about new crises, suffering, and upheavals. This will particularly be true in the legislation I am proposing that would provide for independent monitoring of personal behavior in all our institutions and government structures. I want to tell you about this, but first let me remind you of something very important to consider, which will help us to see the necessity of extraordinary efforts.

Corruption is a part of human behavior and exists in all countries in the world. In our country, at this time, it has reached an unprecedented state. We are no longer a free people. Liberty cannot exist in such corruption. Corruption is a threat to our continued development and in fact has halted and impeded our continued efforts to serve our needs—the needs and rights that are so easily hidden amidst the economic gain and successful activity of the few.

The most important question facing Mexico at this point in our history is how we will face and deal with this great problem. We have allowed it to begin to overpower us and to keep many from eating, working, learning, caring for their families, participating in the benefits of our economy, and living in peace. Let us be reminded that our history is a story of great strength and determination—a story that encourages us to continue to work for peace and justice. When we think of what has been important in our history, what has helped lead us to the great nation that we are, we do not think of governments and organizations. We think of individuals and the great efforts that they have made. It is individual behavior that is at the foundation of our actions.

The new legislation that I am proposing is nothing new. It is, however, a focus on the individuals who are corrupt, who perpetuate corruptness, or who in any way deliberately contribute to the evil of corruption—and in particular those who support illegal activity directly or indirectly related to the drug trade. We shall continue to combat this evil in every way that we can through the legal use of force and control, but increased resources will be made available to form an independent organization that will investigate and pursue corrupt individuals, both in the public and private sectors. This organization will help us in our efforts. We all must continue to support one another in our good efforts and especially in our families, encouraging and teaching the values of personal behavior that we as Mexicans are proud of and that have made us the great nation that we are. It should not be a difficult reminder that all Mexicans have a responsibility to one another to report serious illegal activity to the authorities.

It is especially important for the government to acknowledge the multiple problems of the many youth in our country without hope of future education and work, who are very vulnerable to the influence of corruption. We must deal with this in a new way. This must be a priority of your government, and we are planning new programs to address this great problem.

The following might be some of the most audacious things that you have ever heard from a president of the Republic, but I see the need to say them at this time. The government of Mexico is not responsible for your happiness, nor is it your saviour. The government is responsible to protect your happiness and wellbeing, and it is your servant. It is part of the legal system operating under our constitution, our pact together to serve one another in the pursuit of happiness. The legal system, of which our constitution is part, is our refuge, and we must use it as such. It must be free from corruption, and it must be protected and honoured if we are to work together. We, together, are Mexico.

I am now asking that every Mexican consider how he or she, as well as their family members, friends, and fellow Mexicans are adversely affected by corruption or involved in it, and consider this in terms of what I am telling you. For some, this will be how you are contributing to evil that is destroying your life, the lives of your family members, the lives of your friends and fellow Mexicans. I say this knowing that we must begin to change our attitude, which at times, for some of us, seems one of passive acceptance of corruption—to an attitude that promotes active, assertive behavior that will bring about the needed change in our country—the change that will stop the evil ones from robbing us of our heritage. We must escape from their hold on us, and we must do this together; if necessary, confronting and legally pursuing the justice we have a right to.

I will end by acknowledging that some of what I have said in this speech is an introduction to ongoing weekly presentations. The recent planning meetings essentially consisted of a comprehensive review of the current effects and causes of corruption, with particular attention to the evil of the trade of drugs, which is at the base of many of our problems. This topic will be the start of my presentation and talks with you. My intention, my talking to you in a new way, is to bring a greater awareness or reminder of the gravity of our situation and how we may begin to turn things around.

We are painfully aware of the suffering, injustice, violence, and horrors of the evil and corruption that stems from personal behavior and how some rely upon this for their most basic needs. Even a cursory glance at the arrogant flaunting of the decadent and lavish lifestyle of the so-called drug lords gives us a painful reminder of the gross injustice that we suffer. The active challenge to this injustice will no doubt bring about more suffering, but we must combat it. Part of our challenge is to help one another through what is going to be a very difficult time.

The explorations and reviews undertaken by the government, which have been very seriously criticized by many, have brought me new insights into how I might begin to look at a solution to our individual and collective crisis. It is my hope that by reviewing these things with you and giving greater opportunity for all Mexicans to hear from our teachers among us and our fellow Mexicans from all walks of life, we all may gain insights into what we might all do as individuals and in our collective actions—in our organizations and institutions.

I am asking you to consider this and invite you to watch and listen to the upcoming broadcasts.

The evil that is in our midst has become so prevalent that we base much of our planning and action on it. We must be patient with ourselves and others. Changes will come slowly and, first, with a change of attitude and a sense of concern for others.

I look forward to meeting with you next week and introducing you to others who will speak to you as well as inform you of why my government—your government, our government—is exploring and planning in order to bring to you what is the most beloved thing in the whole universe: equanimity with justice. Then we can begin to live in peace and enjoy the many benefits that life has to offer us.

I rejoice in the great strength, honour, and beauty of Mexico and Mexicans. Our individual loving acts in pursuit of our own wellbeing are the basis of our collective and reciprocal wellbeing. Thank you for your kind attention and your close consideration of what I have spoken to you about today.

11

THE EMPTY PIÑATA

Hope amidst Ridicule

Emptiness, which is conceptually liable to be mistaken for sheer nothingness is in fact the reservoir of infinite possibilities.
—D.T. Suzuki

The week following my speech brought the expected reactions and some unexpected ones. The voices of those who understood and accepted what I was doing were barely heard, nor were they reported in the media. I was not discouraged; at least I told myself that I was not. Nevertheless, my mind was full of those voices that sometimes create ambivalence and regret for actions taken, those voices that invade our focused reflection. I was tempted to entertain these thoughts. However, I was somehow able to remember that my actions and my words were the difficult and conflictual part of a much greater process that I must and would pursue. The supportive words from María and others, each using "we" in "what *we* were doing," brought to mind a great sense of gratitude to know that I was acting, at least in some very important aspects, together with others, out of a pure motive and as one who *saw* the need for action.

The words of my dear friends Héctor and Isabel came to me as I continued to read and contemplate. I became keenly aware that many great educators of the world who write about government, leadership, and power held in common many of the same ideas and were closely linked with what Héctor and Isabel were attempting to teach us. I of course had heard these teachings before. I now recalled the words of my educators in university expounding on political theory and the practice of what the great thinkers had to say about these things. I remembered too the lengthy discussions that we had had about ethical political practice and the dynamics of authentic political leadership and the need for change. I had then recognized the truth of these teachings, but I and many others, it seems, had failed to take them as our own. I was engulfed in living with decisions of what I believed to be the correctness of the balance of power and the permanence of the status quo. I was truly a part of the world of control and tyranny and quite apart from an equitable system—living in my own system of justice that protected me from those whose fate was to serve insatiable need for power and material wealth of the few.

Politicians know of or can often very clearly predict the initial and general reaction to their speeches. Contemplated reactions are considered within the tactic or strategy of every political action. This speech was different. Although I had clearly contemplated what some of the responses would be, my intent did not come with the usual political planning. I knew that there would be a lot of anger, and this was the predominantly initial response to my speech, and it was directed at me and the government. It was the presenting news item in the week following my speech; a constant bombardment of anger and criticism that was most significant. I knew also, before I delivered the speech, that I could not have avoided this initial reaction if I were to very frankly and clearly say what I intended to say.

The media did look beyond this in reporting what I had said, specifically to the current horrendously violent actions and lucrative activities of the drug cartels. However, what it generally commented on, by critical and sarcastic response, was public anger and my failure and the failure of my government to deal with the violence resulting from the drug trade. The media did acknowledge some validity to the solutions to the corruption and violence but indicated what they saw as public opinion—a sense of futility, that the people had given up on the intent and action of government to honestly want to change anything. None of this was unexpected, and I knew that the real work in having the public look beyond the faults of government and to hear what I was saying lay in the implementation of my plan, the upcoming broadcasts.

I was anxious for the start of these broadcasts, which I hoped would bring new insights not only into what was happening in and to Mexico, but also into the role that personal behavior plays in what happens to us. I thought of the work of clerics who constantly remind us of this and of the elusive results in the realm of the hereafter. I also thought of the influence of teachings and how they might only influence us if we believe them. However, my hope was that the clear and tangible results of our behavior, to be discussed in the first presentation, consisting of a reiteration of the damage that corruption had done to our beloved country, would be more enabling because of the ever-present evidence in the compromised lives of people.

In a strange way, the anger shown by the general public was not discouraging. It gave evidence to the dissatisfaction with which people were living. I chose to see it as a kind of defence and support of what I was attempting to do, as a support to what would no doubt be seen as radical action in what I was about to propose in the upcoming presentations to my fellow Mexicans. The anger shown toward me and my government was what I called in my mind a "valid" or "healthy" anger. The anger shown and reported in the press, which came from those involved in the corruption in our country, I saw as a manifestation of perversion and fear, which threatened the lucrative actions and activities of some.

This perverted anger and fear was manifest in the warnings and threats that came to me and others immediately after giving my speech. I was again reminded of the evil that we were dealing with, and I knew that my life and lives of countless others were threatened by this perversion. It was evident that the anger, warnings, and threats came not primarily from the cartels and other criminals, but from those who support them and hide in the impunity that comes with being a public official. The cartels and others who involve themselves in this very lucrative but perverted crime of the drug trade do not have the same fear as those in public positions do; yet the cartel members continue to rely upon those in public positions who are corrupt. It is well known that many powerful people create and support impunity and avoid not only the retaliation from the dreaded drug barons, but from others who support this corruption. Many of them hide in the structures of our social and, more specifically, our political institutions. They have great power to enact upon the tyrannical ambitions that come with ascribed power fuelled by greed and corruption.

The fear that comes with the challenge to change was very much in evidence in the reaction to the speech. It was a challenge to change what was ignored by many, but not by those whose perverse actions clearly illustrated what needed to change if we were to escape the results of corrupt personal behavior.

Among the calls I immediately received after giving the speech was one from Cardinal Contreras. He had been a reluctant participant in the secret meetings. As he expressed concern for my wellbeing and the safety of my family members, his past words came to me: "I'm not sure that this will be productive. We can certainly justifiably confront corruption, but some things simply can be seen and taken into account but must be accepted for what they are." I think that he was indeed concerned for my safety; he is a good person. He is, however, a strong part of the resistance to change that still holds great influence in Mexico and helps to hold us captive to ancient and corrupt powers as well as primitive practices. His concern was certainly mixed with fear of the threat of change to his personal position, in what I was now calling "the *Old* Mexico."

"The church cannot support much of what you said in your speech," he said.

My curt reply was perhaps uncalled for and not entirely true, but I told him, "I was not expecting that it would...The church teaches personal responsibility, but pays little heed to teaching us how to involve ourselves in a transformative process other than feeling guilty about not doing what we are told we should be doing."

I felt a distinct sadness after his call and for my words. I wanted to invite him to be a part of the small group that was supporting my efforts. He is a person who has dedicated his whole life to the service of others. However, he is so entangled and held within the abusive authority of the organized church, which keeps telling us that it is not a democracy. He is lost in belief and obedience that seems to cut him off from compassion and the consideration that enabling wisdom aimed at contributing to human quality of life might come from any source beyond the church. This *monopoly* on truth holds him like a prisoner to rigid action, as it also holds so many others who are trapped in the same prison.

In Mexican culture, we used to have certain things that we simply did not criticize, out of respect. They were like "sacred images" that one simply did not discuss in a negative way. The president, the army, and the Virgin of Guadalupe were known as the three untouchables. One could criticize anything in Mexico, but not the three untouchables, *Los Trés Intocables*. The one remaining untouchable is the Virgin of Guadalupe. The others have long since been abandoned, to be replaced in certain areas of Mexico with things such as mothers, guitars, the flag, Mexican food, music, indigenous heritage, and other important things in Mexican culture. After reading and listening to the response to some of the things in my speech, I sarcastically thought to myself that there was now a *replacement* untouchable. *"The piñata has replaced the president as one of the untouchables,"* I thought.

The piñata is indeed a strong symbol of Mexico, and the media took advantage of my usage of it in my speech. The media employed it to emphasize the negative reaction to my speech. I was called "The Empty Piñata President" by some. Many cartoons depicted me as striking at or glaring at a piñata. One showed the caricatures of many of my cabinet ministers tumbling out of a piñata as I continued to hit it. In every newspaper headline, in every newspaper article, in every newscast, and in the daily conversations throughout the Republic, the piñata was mentioned in relation to government actions and my speech. Although some of the talk of the piñata was a form of light-hearted fun, it nevertheless trivialized and poked fun at what I had said in my speech and of course detracted from the importance of my words, or perhaps added to them in a sense.

This very powerful metaphor brought strong reactions. The use of the empty piñata phrase was so popular that it became applicable to many other situations. Even children were yelling, "Empty the piñata! Empty the piñata!"—totally changing the meaning but thinking they had picked up a new rallying cry to use at various celebrations where the piñata was featured. They shouted the phrase when they were masked and led to hit at it to release the treats it held. For a while, the empty piñata cry became not unlike a rallying cry and response for any cause, especially toward things that were seen as futile or irrelevant, or simply as ridicule for any authority and, especially, the presidency.

"The empty piñata! The empty piñata!" The empty piñata somehow seeped into the constant and pervasive dialogue in my mind, and often, when I could not easily dismiss it in order to focus on what I was doing; I would play with this very powerful symbol. It seemed to keep me away from the fear of what I was doing, and it brought great meaning to me when coupled with the powerful principle that healthy development and change is only built upon the positive. The beautiful piñata served as a sustaining thought for me: Mexico and I would begin to restore and renew a healthier functioning and a more authentic life, that which is on the inside, and bring forth the alignment of this meaning with the piñata's exterior appearance. It is only beautiful if it is filled with good things. It is important not for what is on the outside but what is in the inside.

12
REFLECTIONS

Strength in Planning With Those We Love

> *Most people believe the mind to be a mirror,*
> *more or less accurately reflecting the world outside them,*
> *not realizing on the contrary that the mind*
> *is itself the principal element of creation.*
> —Rabindranath Tagore

A profound feeling of sadness mixed with longing came to me as I contemplated the next step in my plan. These mixed emotions came with thoughts of events and situations in the past, present, and future. It was a paradoxical positive sadness and longing, as it was leading toward joy. These mixed emotions, I thought, came as a result of reflection on the violence, corruption, and tyranny that existed in our country, but also because I somehow knew that I was doing what I should be doing. The experience of these emotions seemed to confirm what I must do and continue to do. I was acting out of a kind of wisdom that comes with correct action that is in harmony with personal values and our action in the world of others. It is a rare thing for me, and even the feelings were difficult to describe. I wondered if I might sustain this and break away from past behavior, which was in alignment with the tyranny that I have recently been confronting in myself and that is also so much a part of how my beloved country functions.

My mind returned again and again to these feelings of sadness and longing, but now with a clearer sense of the joy that they alluded to. This sense of joy came as I began again to discuss and plan with the people who were now lovingly and courageously aligned with me in support and in the practical application of a plan.

This plan and its initiation was not considered seriously by the people of Mexico. My speech was laughed at and ridiculed as an empty political appeal, as an empty piñata. I only hoped that the next aspect of the plan, the evaluation or assessment of Mexico's situation, would create some credibility in what I was doing and an openness to continue to listen to what would follow. I would start with the first of several broadcasts sharing with the nation "The Review of the State of the Nation," followed by the introduction of educators and others who would present what I hoped would bring about the start of the change that we so desperately needed.

I knew too that the conflict that my speech brought about might well increase in multiple proportions as I continued with the broadcasts. I was fearful—not so much of the reaction from the general populace, but from retaliation from corrupt government officials who support the drug cartels. The drug cartels are powerful and are to be feared, but the corruption that is a way of life and that comes from those who rely upon protection by impunity and the lack of transparency in official government organizations was what was to be feared the most in this situation. This power can sabotage any political action that threatens it. Corruption and greed, coupled with nepotism, is an enemy to be feared, especially when it controls so many aspects of Mexican life. It is their power that also gives life to the drug cartels, and their efforts could well bring about open revolt, hidden in an appeal to the populace to oppose my "empty piñata" plan. In this regard, my thoughts turned to how I would respond to the retaliation.

I was reminded that a very powerful and fundamental principle operates in the practical application of our values. While we need to cite what is wrong and ill-conceived, development and change are only brought about by building upon the good, not by combative destructive action that does more harm. I worried about the ongoing practical application of my plan and how I would deal with the conflict and the resulting violence that would surely come with this. How would I act without causing more harm, without causing more harm than good? It would be difficult, but I knew that force would be necessary in defence. I did not hold much trust in those who control our armed forces, nor in the many who show no mercy or compassion if they are opposed. Ultimately, much of this was out of my control. I head the armed forces of

Mexico, but they are feared and often overreact to opposition and do great harm to people.

As I thought about dealing with the conflict and retaliation that would inevitably be brought about by the talks, I also realized that in addition to exerting any control, it too might well be compromised by corruption. I also remembered the comments about the possible retaliation from the drug cartels, which were made by some of the non-governmental participants in "The Review of the State of the Nation." Participants representing students, human rights groups, educators, and clerics repeatedly reminded us that this was a result of fear—a fear that was a reaction to what was perceived as a threat to corruption. It was a fear that resulted in conflict and violence in defense of corruption. They reminded us that it is a necessary aspect of change, and I took refuge in this thought, knowing that I must proceed and not be intimidated by what was a false retaliatory defense of a corrupt system.

Many of my thoughts in those days were also of the awareness of evil in our midst and how I and all Mexicans have been affected by this. Generally, people are aware of the possibilities of horrible occurrences in their lives and in the lives of those they love, but to live with the near and real threatening aspect of this daily is debilitating. The evil was so close to us. It surrounded us, we were part of it. We Mexicans play with death. We know that this is inevitable; but we do not play with evil. We fear it and run from it and, at times, unfortunately, we succumb to it in many ways; thus we live with it, and we are always aware of it. This destructive awareness of evil is part of our lives in Mexico, and it affects everything we do. I wondered how much damage had been done by constantly living with the awareness of this, and in many cases the awareness that one has succumbed to corruption. Living with this is a heavy burden of enslavement.

My growing awareness of being a part of this profoundly affected me in many ways. It is one thing to act in ignorance, but when we become aware of destructive views and behavior, it is like living a lie. We need to know what to do about this awareness. We need to know how to respond. I would emphasize this by reiterating the findings of the review of the sorry state of our nation. I remembered something Isabel said in one of our discussions: "Educators who simply present information are failing if they do not show the relevance and the use of what they are presenting. All education offers the opportunity to improve the quality of life in some way." I knew that "a way out" would be part of what Hector, Isabel, and the other educators would present. I would bring awareness by sharing "The Review of the State of the Nation" with all Mexicans, but I would heavily rely on the educators and others to create motivation, understanding, and a will to engage in dialogue as well as a will to change.

~~~

What a great gift to plan with those who are focused on the task at hand and who are concerned with the task as the primary aspect of collective action and not as part of a tactic that one might only agree with as a partisan plan or a hidden personal plan motivated by power or material gain. What a difference to plan with those you love and trust.

Immediately after my speech, I met with "my team," as Doña Margarita was calling it. All had made a commitment to be with me and support me in the ongoing presentations, providing resources, advice, and personal support as well as their participation in the broadcasts. I gratefully welcomed this. I strongly relied upon all and particularly upon Héctor and Isabel to review and criticize what I presented as my plan.

Diego and Marta Ana were unable to come to this meeting, but they sent their greetings and expressed ongoing commitment. I spoke to Marta Ana on the telephone just before our meeting. I was concerned with their safety. Their absence triggered fear. Apparently they were well and assured me that we need not be concerned. All of the members of the team had been pressured and even threatened with death if they continued to involve themselves in their support of me. Anything out of the ordinary brought great concern for their safety. The absence of Diego and Marta Ana reminded us of the ever-present threat to and the dangerous involvement of my family and friends. I was also reminded that in spite of the ridicule and rejection of my speech, which were attempts to dismiss the intent, the threats showed that those involved in any way with corruption were also indeed fearful. They detested and feared that which sought to defeat them. They feared and attempted to hide this fear in their ridicule and threats.

We all lived within an atmosphere of fear, even the destructive evil ones.

We live in fear of one another and of the threat to our conflicting efforts.

I clearly remember that it was a little disconcerting to have honest dialogues and make decisions with others who so well understood and saw the same needs for Mexico. I remember thinking in the meetings that my lingering fear of hidden agendas, years of defensive partisan presentations, and anguishing difficulties planning with politicians resulted in strange feelings upon working with others who are not competing for personal gain. I reminded myself of the great gift that I had in these individuals. How much I had changed my way of thinking about things; now I thought of the practical application of my values, as opposed to defensive, emotional responses in protection of a way of life that was primarily selfish. It is within the context of my relationship, my unity with them, that I have begun a more authentic life. It is a life in which I am no longer preoccupied with the war within, but deal with this in facing the inner conflicts and the conflicts that present themselves in our outer life with others in a way that is hopeful. I remember thinking that I had spent most of my life fighting with opposing forces within myself and thinking about what I should do instead of what I *was* doing. This seems a part of normal emotional activity within. However, it seemed to me that when we deal primarily with conflict in the world outside ourselves, it adds to the inner division and does not give much room for authentic self-determination.

I was reminded of the changes in how I reflected on things, and I was pleased with this. It is within the context of people such as this, and their courageous efforts, that Mexico will be brought out of the tyranny of corruption and greed. It is within the context of unity, of recognizing the practical application of the principle of unity, and in the positive results of this unity that we can truly individually develop. It is the power of this kind of unity that will face and defeat the fear that surrounds us.

13
THE PRESENTATIONS

Supportive Witness to Our Needs

> *Don't you see, my fellow Mexicans?*
> *This president is trying to tell us how to live*
> *so we can be happy and protect our families...*
> *We must listen. We must stop our corrupt ways.*
> —Don Pedro Alfaro Ruiz

The weekly broadcasts began amidst the ongoing cries of "empty piñata," the ongoing cries of ridicule, threats, denouncements, and destructive criticism. In addition to "the empty piñata," there was also a new cry. It clearly showed a deviant unified effort; a highly sophisticated and orchestrated attempt to create more fear in all Mexicans in a call for the renunciation of my presidency. However, this did not come from "all Mexicans," as was widely reported. The alliance of all those who stood to lose power in their lucrative and corrupt dealings was very strong. They managed to organize and present what seemed like calls from a majority of Mexicans. They promoted a fear that the government was losing economic control, thus adding to the suffering of millions of Mexicans, especially those who live below the poverty line, which is about half of the Mexican population. This was presented in the press in a way that did indeed cause added concern to many, especially the very poor and powerless. It was part of a campaign that sought to discredit and stop what they saw as the next step in the great threat to their continued corrupt and lucrative success.

The corrupt ones, particularly those working within the government and government agencies, greatly feared the presentation of the "Review of the State of the Nation." It made them more vulnerable to being exposed. In Mexico, we have an old saying whose meaning remains in spite of the modern regard for animals: *"Donde hay perros, hay pulgas."* Where there are dogs (the cartels), there are fleas (those who support and gain from the corrupt efforts of the cartels). The "fleas," the corrupt supporters, who hide amidst the corruption and are not easily seen, feared exposure. The review clearly cited these "fleas," and this held great and fearful significance for them. They too live in fear. They too are not exempt from irrational retaliation from the cartels who expect their corrupt alignment; when it is not forthcoming, even by default, they too will be punished, often losing their lives or the lives of their families. These "fleas" live in fear of being detected and killed.

Added to "the empty piñata" cries were, "The president must go" and "The Empty Piñata President must go." It was at this time that international attention to what I was doing increased, and while many groups lauded the efforts, most international political leaders were only mildly expressing concern, particularly those in the US and Canada. Both were obviously pressured by big manufacturers who were fearful of the loss of inexpensive operations in our country. Both countries were continuing to build gigantic manufacturing operations in the industrial zones of the major northern cities, providing jobs for Mexicans but at about one-tenth the cost of what they would pay their own national workers. While this situation might well be seen as a part of the process of development, it was clearly exploitive. These large manufacturers operate like the cartels. They constantly remind my government that they are supplying jobs to poor Mexicans, and we continue to accommodate this exploitive situation, held captive by the actions related to the priorities of capitalistic corruption and crime and not devoting attention to authentic development.

As I write this, I wonder at my discernment and description of this situation. I wondered at times if my theory on the state of Mexico, the state of most of the world, was that "Everything is wrong...everything is mis-developed." How can I be hopeful of the human condition in terms of authentic development and what might improve the quality of our lives? My thoughts were verging on the edge of despair; however, they brought me to contemplate a new idea of the reason for our existence, which left no room for despair. It left only room for hope and continued effort, and I wondered how I had come to this and other thoughts that seemed to take me so far beyond the practical aspects of the contemporary explanations of reality.

~~~

María's comments, just before the first of four presentations reiterating "The Review of the State of the Nation," were meant to be reassuring. In a way they were, but mixed with a certain foreboding. Even if the nation accepted the fact that the government was admitting that it was a part of the corruption, Mexicans, like many peoples who carry residual memories of having been socialized to feel false guilt, do not readily articulate real guilt, nor are they comfortable with others doing so. This is sometimes indicated in a show of over-defensiveness and in dismissing the admission of others who indicate genuine contrition for truly regrettable acts.

How would the nation respond to what María had called "a general confession"? "I think," she said, "reading modified parts of this review in The Official Journal of the Federation is one thing, but to have the president publicly declare that his deceptive government is and has been corrupt and has been stealing from its people is quite another."

I tried to dismiss the inadmissible and the anxiety that I was experiencing because of this. I reminded her that the section indicating Government Policy and Corruption comes at the end of the report, and that I would be reiterating the findings in the order that we reviewed them in the government review.

However, María was correct. She was reminding me of a very basic trait of Mexicans. The admission by the president of the Republic of such horrendous corruption within the government was unheard of in our country. While the truths of this corruption were well known, to say this publicly would not only bring anger but it might also bring a sense of shame and frustration to many, even in contemplation, and before the words were forthcoming from me. In spite of the horror of the drug-related corruption, this admission, with the attention of the international community, would bring Mexicans even more shame.

It was this that many were reacting to after my first broadcast. It dealt with the source, use, and distribution of drugs in Mexico. These are things that Mexicans are very well aware of. It was not the content of these presentation so much as the fact that it was acknowledged publicly that many were reacting to. The angry responses to the broadcasts, in addition to the generalized anger that was part of the empty piñata phenomenon, continued, and as they continued, the inevitable forthcoming comments came: "This Empty Piñata President of the Republic is shaming Mexico and Mexicans."

The second part of the report seemed to bring even more anger, threats, and violence. In addition to dealing with the origin, operation, and escalation of the violence and corruption as well as the use of firearms, human trafficking, and smuggling, it dealt with the massive, lucrative, and destructive activities of the major cartels. The cartels and their supporters reacted to this. With the various cries of "empty piñata," "shame," and "Get rid of this bastard president," a new and interesting aspect became evident. It was denial. There were now comments denying the extent of the problems and particularly denying of the extent of the activities of the cartels. This indicated that they were now acknowledging the seriousness of what we were doing. This denial, and the appeal to accept this idea, was an example of the reliance of the corrupt ones on the support of Mexicans who do not oppose them. Many Mexicans turn a blind eye to corruption and especially to the evil ones. Many of those who live in dire poverty support—and some literally worship—some of the drug lords, both the living and the dead. They are seen as heroes and saints by some. The drug lords often give large amounts of money to individuals and communities who are not even working under their corrupt rule. The perversity of viewing notoriety as popularity seems to elude not only the evil ones, but also the victims of their crimes and deception. It seems that the perverse generosity on the part of the evil ones is a part of a public relations strategy; as María once sarcastically pointed out, it was similar to partisan activity aimed at gaining a similar kind of popularity and at getting votes.

The "shaming of Mexico and Mexicans" and the denial of the immensity of the problems we have with corruption and violence brought me thoughts of how this very complicated situation could cause such confusion and such diverse reactions. While these accusations came from the source of corruption and greed, they were like tactics to protect their actions when presented to the general public, who, in confusion, with doubt, with fear, and in ignorance of the true nature of the corruption, support their accusations.

While shaming Mexico and the Mexican people might well be a result of my actions, this sense of shame comes without knowing the true nature and power of the tyranny of corruption and the corrupt ones and is a false sense of shame. Most Mexicans are the victims of corruption, not only by past events in our unique history; now they are being held and manipulated by the current corrupt ones. Even those who once genuinely aspired to serve them and who now are part of this great conspiracy are now attempting to control them. It is such that the control of public opinion is now also victimized by this corruption. In spite of my growing awareness of just how complicated and massive the situation was, brought about by the corruption in our country, the need to educate Mexicans on how to begin to deal with this brought added certainty of the need for what I was attempting to do. I knew that I must continue.

What I was attempting to do was like a small voice in comparison to the general reaction—or at least was presented in the media and other sources as small. This was to change during the second part of my broadcasts.

The surprisingly new responses were not so much in response to the broadcasts as they were from longstanding efforts to improve the quality of life through ethics and morality. The broadcasts seemed to act as a catalyst to further activate what had been growing for a long time. There were clear alliances to my intent, and they obviously had been in preparation for some time. I knew of these strong educative movements but not as active voices that now began not only to advocate on a national basis, but also to work in similar presentations to inform and educate Mexicans of the state of our country in relation to the intrinsic destructive corruption.

Students and their educators often know the danger of clearly stating truths, especially if they are in conflict with the misuse of power, politically or by big business. Students and student protest movements are often convenient victims of retaliation and violent reprisals in Mexico. It is often like an attack on innocence because guilt looks for a convenient victim, as a means to stop the threatening declarations of injustice. The courageous efforts made by these groups and many others who were forming and working in alliance with combatting the evil acted with great risk. In addition to protests, many universities were starting courses in Corruption and Leadership and forming extraordinary study and work groups, with the intention of educating and practically applying efforts to combat the corruption.

Fundamentalist Protestants, who are known in Mexico as "Christians," were uniting from all over the country to declare alliance with my efforts and forming various spiritual and educative groups. Pastors were urging their church members to take a pledge not to be involved in any activity that was drug related, including businesses and services known to have drug connections. This was a very risky and powerful stance. Although similar efforts also began to take place in the Catholic parishes, the hierarchy remained silent. Many Catholic parishes joined in the activities of the Christian communities, placing themselves in the same position of risk.

The small voice of the "Empty Piñata" was at least being heard. The valiant efforts of many small voices were beginning to bear witness to the corrupt horror in which we lived. In addition to the ongoing conflict and violence from within the world of the evil ones, the retaliations continued, creating increased fear and victimization. No one was exempt from the horror of corruption and death or the threat of death, especially those who opposed and named this evil for what it was. The many invited speakers who joined me in discussion and comments in the broadcasts were receiving daily threats and were now living very different lives, fearful for themselves and their families.

Many journalists were killed for bravely reporting on the activities of the drug cartels. They often named people and prepared excellent reports on the effects of the drug trade. Many of these reports formed a part of "The Review of the State of the Nation." My presentation of these facts in the third round of broadcasts brought a lot of attention from the media. The responses now included more comprehensive reports of what my broadcasts were all about. Many were sympathetic and even began to indicate that this "Empty Piñata" effort might be a serious and different attempt, not simply part of a partisan political plot. This alliance reminded me of the strong educative aspect of journalism and the power that this held, but it was now being attacked even more for acknowledgment of my attempts.

The outcries from many of the more outspoken in my political party were even beginning to wane. My insistence on a comprehensive review of our situation, "The Review of the State of The Nation," had originally been met with resistance from some members of my cabinet. This resistance had now turned to warnings and suggestions how I might modify my broadcasts in some way. Many were now also facing pressure from various sources and even death threats.

Parents and caregivers in Mexico form great lines of vehicles at the end of a school day to pick children up as they leave the school buildings. The process of bringing out children and then linking them with their parents at the end of the school day is a kind of ritual in Mexico. It is so nice to see the parents and children saying their good-byes or running to meet their parents at the end of the day. One day, the husband of one of my cabinet members, an outspoken advocate of what I was doing, was shot at upon his children's exit from school. Moises and his children managed to escape injury, but the seven-year-old daughter of one of the teachers at the school was shot through the head as she inadvertently ran into the gunfire intended for Moises. This was one of so many horrific acts of violence aimed at retaliation and prevention of further action on my part in continuance of the broadcasts.

This new violence was now part of the ongoing viciousness that was intrinsically related to the corruption and violence that was a way of life—violence we try to avoid and fear to create in our confrontation of evil in our midst. It was the conflict and violence that often kept us from action. It was this violence and conflict that created false guilt and ambivalence. The support of María and all the others who courageously added to what I was doing kept me from what in the past would have been long and damaging thoughts about the creation of this conflict because of my actions and in the promotion of the actions of others.

The regret I now felt was not guilt. It was the regret that comes from the damage caused by others who oppose equanimity and freedom and the ensuing conflict and violence that is created in opposition to this evil that holds us so tightly in its threat to totally destroy us. It seeks to destroy us whether or not we continue to feed its insatiable greed by collaborative participation in corruption.

The fear that this created never really left my mind, but it had not yet overwhelmed me to the point of experiencing the false guilt that can come in such a terrible situation. I was, however, very close to this as I contemplated our problems of corruption. The complex nature of responsibility in the face of evil is always somehow related to our personal actions. I was taught to avoid or appease the conflict that leads to justice for others, and now my conscience told me otherwise, but with great fear of the interim consequences of my actions.

It is the first responsibility of a leader to protect the people, but it is not always a clear path to that security. It seems like the path of martyrdom, whose meaning I once ignored, because it so eluded me.

14

DIEGO

Great Anguish in Sacrifice

...rid of earthly contagion.
—Post-Communion Prayer, *Mass for the Dead*

I relied on brief notes from my diary to give memory to the progression of events that I am writing about here. My last entry was made following one of the most painful and disturbing events of my life. There was a gap of about three months in my diary. The lack of written words somewhat reflected my life during that time. I was almost devoid of words, and at times devoid of clear concepts. The words, the cognitive reflection and planning, and the wondering and worry, the judgments, the consciousness of being aware of and focused upon what was happening within and without, was totally overwhelmed and at times crushed by emotion. I even now find it hard to identify or articulate this, except to say that it was part of an overwhelming grief that held me very firmly. Often people say that they are unable to identify their emotions. I now have a better understanding of this. I comment on all of this now as a way of delaying articulation of the painful event that precipitated this, but which I now painfully reveal.

My brother, Diego, his wife, Marta Ana, and their grandchild, Olivia were brutally murdered as they left a restaurant in downtown Guadalajara. They were riddled with gunshot wounds and left to lie in their blood for more than an hour at the entrance of the restaurant, their martyred bodies abandoned because of fear. It was difficult to determine the source of the gunshots, and until the authorities were able to search the surrounding buildings, they were afraid to go near and remove the bodies. The evil ones had claimed more victims in retaliation.

The inconsolable grief and anguish that I experienced for these several weeks eventually turned to guilt, anger, and bitterness. Somehow I gradually returned from a state of hollowness and then to a state of relative calm.

I am still attempting to recapture my desire to be compassionate and again accept the things that I have learned from my reflections and my teachers. I have begun to make room in my hollowness for a sense of gratitude that I survived some of the pain and for the patience and understanding of my close others, especially María. I know that the first and strongest positive emotion that I began to feel after Diego's death was gratitude, because of the kindness shown to me and María. This feeling eventually lead to the other emotions I am now beginning to feel. I am still very far from feeling any joy in any situation.

The hollowness of my grief, which turned to guilt, bitterness, and anger, was seen only by others as bitterness and anger. It was assumed that this was primarily directed at and the result of the actions of others—the crime, the corruption, and the corrupt ones. Some of it was, but it was primarily self-directed and reached a kind of despair that I knew would end only in more and increased anguish. However, in a strange way, in the atmosphere of violence and the emotional atmosphere that surrounded us at this time, which we lived with every day in Mexico, I really did not see that I was directing this guilt, bitterness, and anger at myself. María did see this, and the quality of her love and keen discernment in breaking this I will never forget.

In a quiet moment without too many words, which was the usual context of our relationship at this terrible time of grief, she suddenly and quietly said, "I know that you are feeling guilty for the death of Diego, Marta Ana, and Olivia. I know too that this is false guilt. It is the false guilt that you have so feared and that comes as the result of conflict in correct action. You have not escaped this horrible false emotion, and you must break away from it."

Even though I did not really understand why, I initially only really heard the names of Diego, Marta Ana, and Olivia. I was so hurt by just by hearing the names and then by her comments that I was unable to respond. *How could she, at a time like this when we are in such horrible pain, say such a thing?*

I did not really hear what she said, but I began to think about her words, and I began to do something that I rarely do. I cried. The tears brought forth a release so profound that I trembled.

María was right. I was holding on to something that was not there. I became very cognisant of the fact that I was not guilty of any deliberate harm, although it was clear that this horrific act was done in retaliation. I was *not* guilty. I was *not* responsible for the cruel acts done by the evil ones in retaliation. I was *not* responsible for the death of Diego nor the deaths of husbands and wives, brothers and sisters, sons and daughters, mothers and fathers—all those who were targeted for non-alliance or for not participating in collaborative evil efforts.

The significance of the dynamic of the creation of false guilt was not easy to relinquish. I could not easily leave the thoughts that came to me. My actions were not the primary cause of the retaliatory violence, but they were indeed what had precipitated some of the violence. I detested the thought of creating martyrs.

My thoughts extended to the thousands of soldiers all over the world who are sent to war each year. The evil we do to one another is so monstrous, so far reaching, and so complicated. It occurs and grows in multiple proportions that often obscure the cause, except that it is always a result of individual or collective personal behavior. This evil does not easily leave my mind for long, especially in contemplation of the effects of retaliation and the continued action that I know I must continue to take.

Some of the false guilt remains as a residue in my thoughts, to come repeatedly like the evil ones do. The faces of Diego, Marta Ana, and Olivia come to me now along with my thoughts, and along with all the faces of all those who have suffered and died because of the actions of the evil ones. They come to me with peaceful regard, but part of me sees then as a haunting. There is no refuge from this aspect of my thoughts. My thoughts bring me to, *"How careful we must be in exercising any kind of power over others."*

I don't remember very much of what was said at the funeral mass for Diego, Marta Ana, and Olivia, but a few of the words in one of the readings were very significant to me, and they linger in my mind as I think of Mexico and the victims, living and dead, who suffer from our complicated corruptness.

Referring to those who died as "servants and handmaids," the reading says that they are now "rid of earthly contagion." The words linger with me because I think of the corruption as a kind of contagion that spreads directly or indirectly, bringing the illness that strikes the culpable and the innocent in divergent ways, always lurking, at times unheeded and often hidden from clear view. At times it is even masked and presented as an aid to the quality of life. We live in the midst of this contagion, and we are unable at times to run from it. If we do resist it or fight it, we pay the consequences in brutal retaliation and false guilt for having inadvertently initiated conflict and possible harm to others.

Three weeks following the deaths of Diego, Marta Ana, and Olivia, Don Alberto and his wife, Leticia, were shot to death in their car as they were leaving their home in Mexico City to go to a family gathering in Puebla. The brutal way in which they were killed seemed to reflect the very great anger and hatred that was part of the revenge and retaliation. Their car was riddled with enough bullets to destroy hundreds of people—like many others who were also brutally murdered in other parts of the country during the same week. The graphic photographs of brutal attacks constantly shocked many Mexicans, and this case was no exception. Don Alberto Rodríguez Robles was very well known and respected. The media comprehensively covered not only his and his wife's deaths in great detail, it also told his life story, emphasizing his great contribution to Mexican society as an educator and an advocate for justice.

He had come to Mexico after retiring from the Supreme Court of Spain, where he was highly respected. He became very well known and loved in Mexico for his outspoken but constructive ideas on social reform and justice. He was an advisor to many educators and reformers.

Included in the media coverage of Don Alberto's death and legacy was a lengthy account of his current interest and work, along with a detailed account of the motive for his murder. As one of my chief supporters and part of my core team, there were many accounts of his support of my plan and his efforts and involvement in the planning and presentation in the broadcasts. It was obvious that his murder was a retaliatory vindictive act because of his stance and efforts in support of combatting corruption, and this was clearly cited in many of the reports.

The various media reports of Don Alberto's murder prompted more attention on the various efforts to combat corruption and the drug cartels. Although this attention was not new, it was a constant subject of discussion. In addition to the problem of corruption within the government, many journalists began to talk about the need for education, giving credence to my efforts and the efforts of others who were not well known or recognized. Generally, the need for more structure and force by government authorities and the armed forces was stressed in the battle against these things. The inclusion of education and motivation of Mexicans was a welcomed new emphasis. It brought greater attention to my broadcasts and to all of the other efforts that were beginning to grow with increased interest. Along with this came various and comprehensive reports and articles related to the corruption and violence, including reports of the many Mexicans who were moving to the US and elsewhere to flee the corruption and violence.

The members of the cartels often communicate various vindictive and threatening messages by sending letters to the press, which are often photographed and reported, for the public to see. They also often leave crudely written messages on pieces of cardboard hung around the necks of their dead victims or near the place of their gruesome deaths. The latest messages began to include things that indicated the fear of including an educative aspect in the efforts against their evil. The messages included warnings and sarcastic notes aimed at those who might be in alliance with "The Empty Piñata President," threatening death to me and to all who are in support of my efforts.

My thoughts brought me strange words: *"The evil ones fear awareness and knowledge more than those who only reluctantly embrace these things as effective combat."*

15

THE VERGE OF SADNESS

Carrying On

Never let the future disturb you.
You will meet it, if you have to, with the same weapons of reason
which today arm you against the present.
—Marcus Aurelius, *Meditations*

I can't go on, I'll go on.
—Samuel Beckett

In a review of what I have already written, and as I continued to write this account of my brief time in office and of my personal and professional experience, I felt at a great loss as I began this new chapter. This feeling of loss came at a time when my thoughts were again taking me away from the very clear and practical planning that I was beginning to achieve. The feelings I had were perhaps more of a feeling of lack or of an absence, and it was related to being very mindful of the fact that I can only really give a small picture of who I am and of the thoughts that are the basis of my action, inaction, and development.

I can only give a small picture of the overwhelming corruption and violence that were occurring in Mexico. I could only give a very small picture of the suffering and agony of Mexicans. I could only give a small picture of what has happened, is happening, and will happen to me as president and in Mexico, our beloved country.

I wonder if my words will suffice to capture the essence of these things and be sufficiently meaningful to whoever might read my account. These and other thoughts questioning my path and my actions have returned to me to constantly self-evaluate. This self-evaluation veered toward a threat to the resolve I had of continuing with what I was doing. My thoughts again were often very negative. Nevertheless, a return to compulsive thoughts, which I have been stuck with in the past, has also given some strange credibility to what I am doing, although the thoughts of giving equal credibility and consideration to totally opposing points of view and corresponding possible actions was again with me, or at least within my fleeting and sometimes conflicting thoughts. Some of these were manifest in intense pensive moods where my attention was drawn away by thoughts in a way that was much more extreme than usual.

It is interesting how our minds, triggered by some small event, often bring us to the sublime, to uplifting thoughts. They too can also bring us to the mundane and the ridiculous and keep us in bondage. The thoughts of my inability to truly explain the horror of what was happening in Mexico spiralled and brought me to thoughts of the inadequacy of my plan and again to the false guilt that at times came with this great struggle. I had learned not to cling to the immediate emotional response of my thoughts, but I seemed at this time to lack the resolve to do this, entertaining instead doubt and ambivalence in compulsive thoughts that brought me to the edge of sadness and sometimes close to depression.

I think that what I then saw as a regression in my resolution and plans for Mexico and for myself was brought about by the intensity and abundance of negative events—the horrible loss of life, piling up against us, particularly the murders of Diego, Marta Ana, and Olivia. I was clearly still able to intellectually affirm that I would not let the weakest part of me influence me—the often intense and mixed emotional responses that come from the pressure outside us. I would not let the weakest part of myself change my basic resolve. I knew this. However, the entertainment in my mind of ambivalence and doubt, I now see, was simply allowing myself to mourn and was only vaguely related to despair of my plan. I never really felt clinically depressed or dysfunctional.

Triggered by the deaths of those so dear to me, my pain and regard generalized to the thousands who suffer and die every day in Mexico and who are also mourned by others. I felt a strange but powerful union in this aspect of my mourning, which, in a very strange way, did not allow the luxury of morning only for myself. I truly did feel the pain of my fellow Mexicans, and this, somehow, for me at least, validated the sincerity of my plan and actions aimed at countering and combatting the evil that surrounded us. I continued, in spite of this inner conflict, knowing that if nothing else, the strong intent of my desire to endure and at least try to change things was still intact.

As the weekly broadcasts continued, so did we all. We continued to live what seemed at times, when I was at my lowest ebbs, to be a lie; we rejoiced in the wholesomeness of family life, celebrating, as Mexicans do, our culture and values and enjoying what seemed to be a development of a Mexico that was learning to meet the basic needs of so many of its people. Yet the extent of the poverty and great suffering was really hidden from open view or masked by the joy and celebration that generously takes place in everyday living. I was never able to do this very well, to mask my anger, suffering, and pain in celebration of life. I see now that I have always had the luxury of complaining and options—the possibility of changing my situation—so I have always freely complained and expressed my sufferings.

I learned this in my family and in my social contacts. We had resources. We were free to express our suffering. This is something the poor of Mexico do not have the option of doing. They are held captive in suffering and poverty by those of us who thrive upon them as a resource and in fact keep resources from them. They occasionally explode with anger and rebel, only to be fought with the force of soldiers and law, beaten back to submission. I wondered then, in my negative thoughts, if what I was trying to do was to force them into rebellion by my educative and motivating lectures. Is this how it seemed to others, who saw what I was doing as a threat to their isolated and protected security?

We were doing these things that we usually did, living with the paradox of poor and rich. However, we were all also continuing to suffer from the tyranny and hypocrisy of the myth of the adequacy of our current state and the official actions that hid "1001" manifestations of evil, corruption, and crime. The resulting and ongoing agony we so much wanted to relieve—the violence, the destruction, the killings and decapitations, the recent murder of another cabinet minister and other government officials, and the continued murders of clerics, educators, ordinary people, and others who openly spoke out about our evil and of the devastation of families and friends. The list went on and on. This *status quo* and the acceptance of it while we celebrated life was also our enemy. We needed to learn to hate this kind of complacency and to change it to an authentic celebration of life by combatting and overcoming the evil of our actions.

My episodes of negative thoughts came; more and more taunting me that all that I was doing in my plan was making things worse for all of us. I was causing an uprising in the status quo, and this could not lead to the equanimity and justice that Héctor and Isabel so firmly believed in and that was implied in the lectures and talks we were giving. How could it? I began to doubt again, and it was painful. I wondered if my actions could only lead to more division and violence and the guilt that I would then feel would not be false.

It was a time of living with combative thoughts that I somehow survived, but the thoughts were, I now know, valid considerations. So much of what we do to improve the quality of our lives and the lives of others is very complicated, and the outcome is always hidden from clear view. These and other thoughts came to me, but I was somehow able to leave these more philosophical considerations and continue with the practical aspects of what I was doing in spite of the overwhelming sense of failure that came to me.

The weekly broadcasts continued amidst the horrors and the threats of retaliation. These retaliations were realized in the most brutal ways. As in the case of my speech, feedback from every broadcast came almost immediately from those who were threatened by the content. The press began to seriously review what the presentations offered. Some aligned themselves with comprehensive presentations, not only on the state of the nation in terms of corruption, but many took on the role of educators, presenting very detailed articles on personal and collective behavior, leadership, and the nature of corruption. They discussed various areas that were directly and indirectly related to the drug trade and the corrupt practices of every governmental organization.

These actions of the media and others indicated, in some small sense, the impact of our broadcasts. But nowhere was this more immediately evident than in a talk given by Don Pedro Alfaro Ruiz, an indigenous subsistence farmer from the state of Guerrero, whose whole family had been very directly and horrendously affected by the drug cartels and whose presentation in one of our broadcasts was to bring about an emotional reaction in the country that was truly remarkable. It also brought me to strengthen my resolve a little, and gave me a brief respite from my compulsive thoughts of ambivalence in our efforts.

The state of Guerrero has Mexico's highest murder rate, directly related to the drug trade and its evil actions. It is a very beautiful state but a dangerous place for many. Guerrero was the location, a few months earlier, of the sinister abduction and massacre of an entire cohort of student teachers, along with their professors, a cleric, two nuns, and all of the support staff. Any news from Guerrero at that time meant violence and suffering.

There are many indigenous communities in Guerrero. The people there have worked for centuries as farmers, growing corn and other staples. In recent years, some of the communities have started to plant poppies; it is an ideal place to grow them because of the climate. In this way, many were able to escape the grinding poverty in which they live. They did this not only at great risk because of the law, but more so because of the violent and corrupt competition among those who participate in the drug trade. The harvested gum from the poppies was sold to various drug operations. More than fifty percent of the opium and heroin that is produced in Mexico comes from Guerrero. It is a very lucrative business, and various cartels compete for control of the marketing and the places where the drug is produced. They are in deadly conflict with one another and with the many indigenous communities who oppose other indigenous producers. The locals were in a state of war with one another.

The groups of indigenous who are opposed to the production of the drug have banded together to form *autodefensas,* self-help groups. They were illegally formed and clearly stated that they were attempting to provide what my government did not provide—security and opposition to the drug trade and the ensuing violence and corruption.

Don Pedro spoke of the conditions in Guerrero and of his lost family. He spoke of these things as a humble and defeated *campasino*, and he captured the attention of all Mexicans. Don Pedro was invited to speak on the broadcast by Héctor. I don't know how Héctor knew him, but he convinced us that Don Pedro should speak. He started his talk by saying "We must listen to this Empty Piñata President!" The recording was immediately stopped, but Héctor insisted that we continue to allow Don Pedro to speak, and I ordered the recording team to continue, not knowing what was to come next.

Don Pedro continued to speak, very humbly and clearly. He told us that although he did not totally trust what I was doing, he had confidence that I was at least honest and that we had very little choice but to listen and begin to act like "true Mexicans." He captured the essence of the many words in our broadcast with very few words of his own. It was like the distilled essence of what we were saying. He told Mexicans that what I was trying to do was to remind us how to live and that if we wanted to have families and a life, we must cooperate and not only change our behavior but confront one another, with compassion and love.

He directed his words very clearly to the members of government and government agencies, saying that he thought that the talks were beginning to display the extent of corruption and that individual personal behavior must be cited and dealt with. It was about this time that the special agency that was formed to seek out corrupt members of the government, the armed forces, and any organization was beginning to charge many with corruption and theft. The process was slow, but it was well reported in the media, which helped to give credence to our efforts. Don Pedro was obviously aware of this and said that the actions taken by the government to rid itself of the corruption were beginning to be evident, but he angrily and sarcastically stated that it was too late for his family. He clearly showed the general feelings of disgust at the perceived abandonment by the government, at the same time urging others to acknowledge that things might well be changing.

At one point in the talk, Don Pedro cried and appealed to Mexicans saying, "Don't you see, my fellow Mexicans? This president is trying to tell us how to live so we can be happy and to protect our families." He went on to tell of the loss of his parents, wife, children, and grandchildren in various horrendous ways, all retaliatory casualties because of the drug trade. His wife and one of his daughters were repeatedly raped and then butchered in front of him in retaliation for his resistance to some aspect of his conflictive dealings with the cartels. One of his sons was murdered and his badly bruised and naked, lifeless body was hung upside-down from a tree in the plaza of the village. The rest of his family members were murdered in various ways, except for one son who fell from the back of a truck trying to escape the police. His body was run over by several police vehicles in pursuit. They did not even attempt to avoid this brutal indignation and mutilation of his body. His young grandson witnessed this horror as he screamed from the back of the escaping truck. He too, along with his mother, Pedro's daughter-in-law, and several others who were also in the back of the truck, were later killed in the ensuing shootout.

He told us how he now sits alone in his little house, rejected by most of the community because of his drug involvement, anguishing for himself and for all of Mexico. He said that he often finds it difficult to even believe that every member—ten in all—of his family has been killed as a result of the evil corruption and violence related to drugs. He confessed to having been involved in the illicit growing of poppies. The resulting sale and handling of the drug brought his family members into the activities and eventually to their deaths. His sense of guilt was overwhelming. His simple way of telling his story was compelling.

He told us how he accommodated corruption by overpaying for various things and cooperating with the drug cartels to illegally evict others from their land. Every one of his family members died a violent death as a result of activities related to his involvement in the drug trade.

Don Pedro reminisced about his life before his involvement in the drug trade and how, although desperately poor, he and his family lived with joy and hope, enjoying one another and always looking to others and the government to help them—the help that never came. "Now" he said, "we must listen... we must stop our corrupt ways, and we must rely on this president to help us to stop the corruption of his people. This president will soon be gone, and another who might be worse than he is and not care about us so much will take his place. Let us start a change to get better; a change that cannot be stopped by the next one."

He finished his speech by invoking the Holy Virgin to help Mexico and to have mercy on him in his loneliness, guilt, and sorrow. He ended by saying that this was the first time in many years that he had dared ask the Holy Virgin for something, saying that he was so overwhelmed with shame that he dared not ask God or the Virgin for anything.

~~~

All of Mexico talked about Don Pedro and his speech for several weeks.

His humble words were quoted and used in many presentations by others who were promoting what then seemed like a clearer cause in the appeal to change individual behavior and combat corruption.

In a strange way, Pedro Alfaro Ruiz, an uneducated, illiterate farmer, told us what was going on, educating us in a way that seemed to enable Mexicans to think beyond our suffering and motivate us to be better than we were. Although he supported what the government was doing, what I was doing in the presentations, he put things in perspective by reminding us that we were losing the very things that we loved and enjoyed—our families and friends, our communities, a sense of being a part of life, and even our contact with God. His humble and courageous way of expressing the cause of his suffering and his loneliness impressed many.

I knew that the ongoing effects of emotional reactions are sometimes sustained in action and sometimes, like entertainment, are readily enjoyed but very easily forgotten. However, coupled with the information that was now coming from the weekly presentations, the press, educators and students, various church groups, and others, a union or balance of emotion and facts does in fact have the potential to initiate and support personal change. After the emotional anguish of an issue is dealt with, if it is based in a clearly discernable principle held in common with an intellectual assertion, it is more often liable to remain an issue that will continue to be defended and dealt with.

Don Pedro's humble and frank words held great power. The emotional response throughout the country was evident, with few public manifestations, but with widespread reporting from the media. His story was based in the harsh facts of loss that could not be greater. It was the same loss that Mexicans were dealing with every day and with which they could well relate. Mexican principles, although compromised somewhat in their practical application by the corruption and violence, were still very much intact, and the efforts that we were making, I hoped, were creating a difference. Don Pedro's voice was a powerful catalyst to this search for a way out of the corruption we were mired in; it held the attention of so many, primarily as an emotional appeal.

Mexicans often respond with great enthusiasm to highly charged emotional aspects of various issues that have a basis in justice. This involves something of a paradox in that the great protest of words, rallies, and manifestations are really only a form of forceful complaint and not based on or associated with any strategic plan to forcefully bring about real social change. It is a way to legally and without open conflict protest the injustices without a real threat to those—traditionally the government-protected rich and powerful—who are keeping them from the justice and social needs that they desire. Mexican governments have been aware of this dynamic and even encourage protests, knowing they are simply a release of anguish and not a real threat—like the encouragement of a collective self-defeating and neurotic behavior as an appeasement. I was hoping that the enthusiasm for my plan that was beginning to manifest itself in Mexico was not immersed in this dynamic and that it was a balance of emotion and intellect, which might well bring about real and lasting change. I thought about this as I heard of the impact that Don Pedro's speech had had.

It was about this time that in addition to the confrontations of my own thoughts, additional challenges to what I was doing came in greater force, not only from the evil "dogs and fleas," but also from those within my own government. Many voices were confronting me for my action related to my plan for Mexico. The most pressing were from my political party and my cabinet members. Although many understood and accepted that we needed more concentrated efforts in our fight against the cartels, I was being accused of neglecting the many other issues that were facing Mexico at that time. Very few really understood or were willing to face the immensity of the thinking behind changing the individual personal behavior of the nation and a possible change in the corrupt managing of both government and non-governmental organizations. It was simply beyond the scope of thought for many who were steeped in the political functioning that did not include the conviction or belief that modern leadership necessarily included education, motivation, and a greater regard for the wellbeing of people, apart from being the guardians of the relationship between capitalistic commerce and the production and protection of wealth for those who held power. The truth was that Mexico was doing very well monetarily at this time. Our economy was stable, millions of tourists continued to flock to our country, and the rich were getting richer. The fear manifest in many objections to my plan was not based in fear of economic failure nor the failure of the commonly expected result of political action, but in fear related to equality and justice and the combating of evil with the usual retaliation. Furthermore, there was fear of the unknown aspects, that this might bring a new way of life for Mexicans.

It was about this time that my thoughts turned more and more to the short remaining time that I had in office, and I wondered if this brought some of the ambivalent feelings that I was having about my life and my plan. At times like this I usually arrange—or María reminds me of my need of a break to our beloved Santa Rosa. We had been unable to get away to Santa Rosa for a while, and I was beginning to long for even a weekend respite from the daily grind.

A change of scene often brings not only a change in perspective, but also a change in emotional state. I thought of a trip that I would soon take to Canada. I knew that this would bring me a change and a rest. Although it was to attend a two-day conference, an old and dear friend had invited María and me to spend some time at their home to visit and enjoy a bit of a respite. I was looking forward to this and to a change of pace.

As I reviewed my diary to write this chapter, I saw that I had ended my notes with: "*No voy a permitir que lo desconocido y la tristeza actuar como mi guía.*" I will not allow the unknown and the sadness to act as my guide.

16
MARÍA

Continuing the Effort with Hope and Love

> *What you leave behind is not what is engraved in stone monuments, but what is woven into the lives of others.*
> —Pericles

My name is María—María Ángeles Santos Aguilar. I am Miguel's widow. Upon writing this, a year has passed since Miguel died in a terrible plane crash, along with several other government officials and business people.

I begin this final chapter of Miguel's story to you, as he did—telling you who I am. However, I know that I will find it difficult to clearly explain why I chose to finish his account of his brief time as president of Mexico—I am a reluctant and sporadic writer, and I do not talk objectively about the people whom I love. However, like Miguel, who was encouraged by me and many others to write something of his time as president, I too have been encouraged to write this last chapter, a short epilogue to what Miguel was writing of his past life and as his time as president of the Mexican United States. Our son, Lalo, and his wife, Malena, our daughter, Maribel, and her husband, Nacho, have all encouraged me to do so.

At first we thought that it would be an audacious presumption to "finish" Miguel's work, but we decided that it would not be published otherwise, and we thought that writing something in explanation would help honour the memory of my dear Miguel. We also thought that we would like to say a little about what has transpired following his last writing. We think that Miguel intended to publish his writing, and we also want to honour this. We all agreed that it would be good to comment on Miguel's life and also to offer some kind of conclusion by telling about what has happened in Mexico as a result of Miguel's plan for Mexico, his efforts to combat the intrinsic corruption in our beloved country.

Miguel's reflections and thoughts were done within a brief period of his life, but they include his lifelong search for authentic meaning and action—the greatest gift anyone can give. The period of his presidency was a time of great personal change and of extraordinary circumstances in the political and social life of Mexico and in the greater context of the world situation.

I don't know how much more Miguel had intended to write. I do know that he had not had his work reviewed and apparently was not yet thinking of publishing. Although I encouraged Lalo, who is a professor of literature, to review and modify parts of Miguel's work before I wrote this epilogue, he and Maribel were adamant that it should be left the way it is, adding only my concluding chapter with some explanations of what I thought were appropriate. I had thought that many things were left too implicitly or with implied understanding and that these things should be clarified or at least mentioned. However, I see that Lalo and Maribel were right. They also know that I do not talk without embellishment of the qualities of those I love, and they have warned me about writing too much and not leaving what Miguel said to be seen within the context of the reader's own understanding. I too think that I might write too much, knowing that I will find it hard not to compensate for what I think that Miguel would have us understand. I will leave my over-writing also to the understanding of the reader to see this within the context of my concern for this and my love for Miguel.

What is written in Miguel's work are primarily his thoughts and contemplations. The greater context of some aspects of his thoughts and ideas will be well known to those who understand human behavior and what is happening in Mexico and in the world, as well as the interrelatedness of these things. The details and greater contextual aspects of what Miguel writes about would be self-evident and understood in context, perhaps differently by various individuals, but that is always as it is. I will try to only allude to or briefly explain some things in my brief epilogue and leave to the reader's imagination whether or not I have obscured the qualities that I saw in Miguel because of my emotional involvement.

I always thought that Miguel intended to look to the possibility of continuing to work directly with his plan after his presidency, either as part of his political party or perhaps through education. I now know that this was what he was anxious to talk to me about after his meeting with his old friend from Canada. Miguel kept many notes of various teachings, particularly on leadership and governance, and what appears to be outlines of various writings that he intended to work on at a later time. Lalo has these, and with the help of Héctor and Isabel, he will begin to look through them to see if they might also be used in some way related to education, or in a continuation of Miguel's intent and work related to his plan.

Shortly after completing his last writing, Miguel went to Ottawa, Canada. He brought a delegation of his cabinet ministers and business people to attend a meeting of NAFTA members. Ottawa, the capital of Canada, is a beautiful city that holds many good memories for Miguel. He was pleased to be going, not only as part of his duties as president—he was always enthusiastic about any aspect of his duties, but also because he would be meeting old friends who shared some of his values and ideas.

After the conference, he was invited to spend the weekend with one of the delegates at the conference, his old friend David Lalonde, a former prime minister of Canada. David and his wife, Sally, own a rural home called "Les Arches." It is close to the city of Ottawa. It has become somewhat of a retreat centre for many of David and Sally's friends. Miguel met David when he was a teenager. They and other children of privilege and wealth from various parts of North America attended a summer camp in a rural part of New York State for several years. They formed strong and lasting friendships and often visited one another.

Miguel had been to Les Arches several times. I also have been there and immediately recognized why Miguel called it his Canadian Santa Rosa. I knew that he would find his visit there to be uplifting, and he indeed confirmed this in our telephone conversation the night before he was to return home. He was very anxious to tell me about his visit with David and Sally and some of the discussions and plans that they had. In our telephone conversation, Miguel sent along regards from David and Sally, who also "scolded" me for not coming along on the trip, and a promise to visit with us at Santa Rosa when they could.

I think that Miguel needed a break away from the daily grind of pressure that his job consistently presented. The last entry in his writing clearly indicates that he was at a low ebb and feeling a little overwhelmed.

Thinking back to this time, I see now that Miguel was on the edge of depression. He wanted me to accompany him to Canada, and in our discussion of this, his mood was very different and difficult to discern. I thought that he was simply looking forward to his trip, but I see now that his altered mood was perhaps masking a depression, which he himself perhaps did not recognize.

Miguel's short break away was sustaining and restorative, and I am so grateful for this. I was so looking forward to meeting him at the airport upon his return.

He never arrived. I never saw him again.

The presidential plane went down shortly after leaving Ottawa, in the state of Pennsylvania, killing Miguel and all eleven people who had remained in Ottawa for the weekend. Some of the delegates had returned to Mexico immediately after the conference while the others had planned to return with Miguel on the Monday morning.

We still have, after a year, no definitive answer as to why the presidential plane crashed. Many believe that Miguel and the others were indeed assassinated by one of the drug lords who, shortly before Miguel left for Canada, had sworn to kill him for his war against his "family," but there were many who had threatened his life. The unknown, albeit a very important part, remains a relatively minor part in terms of the great anguish and loss that I will always feel. We live in times where any disagreement that involves power is often dealt with in violence, which dismisses the possibility of collective action that leads to dialogue and peaceful resolution. Some of the violence, of course, is born simply of ill-will and greed.

If Miguel was assassinated, it was because of the madness that is created and fostered by ill-will and greed—the very things that Miguel was attempting to combat in Mexico, his beloved Mexico that is so tightly bound in the pervasive ill-will, greed, and corruption and personal behavior that seeks to even kill in retaliation for ethical action.

Miguel was one of the most intellectually honest people I have known. His search for authenticity and meaning brought him to the firm conviction that evaluation and knowledge of the self was linked to and very closely related to the ongoing occurrences in our lives. He somehow overcame the reluctance and fear that seems to keep many of us from a genuine search in our lives that leads away from the blind alley of belief and enters into a process of transformation. Miguel knew that insight, wisdom, and the reality of life is what makes us truly free. His particular mindfulness was illustrated by his paying attention to these things, along with shedding the beliefs, tenets, and dogmas of organized belief systems. His primary journey was along a path that is transformative, and that leads to liberation and freedom. This is what I think he was trying to tell us.

Miguel also learned not to hold to primary emotional reactions and allow these to blur his personal planning. He was able to deal with his mental dialogue in a way that brought him clarity and security in his convictions. He was wise enough not to allow early learned emotional responses, which often keep us bound to act out of fear, anger, or a sense of helplessness, to hold us in bondage.

As a young person, Miguel was very "Catholic." He was immersed in the great metaphors of the church and found meaning and solace in its words—words and warnings that bring great solace and meaning to those who do not explore their actions beyond belief and who are held by an authority that stresses surrender instead of self-development. These things served him well and were part of his early personal and family culture.

His ongoing search led him, however, to see that these things held very little in terms of his own particular search, and he broke through the primitive concepts, metaphoric language, and comfort of religion to find that he was, like all of us, alone in his search. He recognized the value of using the structures and teachings not as a salvific force, but as a guide to what helps us to reveal to ourselves the truths that lead us on our particular paths and deal with the disagreeable things of life. Miguel still carried vestiges of metaphors of religion, looking for solace in God, the Virgin, and the saints, but whose existence or aid he no longer held as certain.

His assured metaphors, however, held great meaning. Santa Rosa was a very powerful metaphor of love, family, others, respite, rest, insight, and happiness. It was the antithesis of his symbol of "evil" and "the evil ones," which spoke of all that was wrong and in particular those whose personal behavior held Mexico and Mexicans in bondage because of the drug trade.

Miguel's writings seem to mistakenly indicate that he was too driven and pressured in his life search. I do not think that he was. He was persistent. He knew the value of reviewing very basic things and sometimes appeared as if he was compulsively digging up his roots to see if he was growing. He did, however, seem to allow his thoughts to enter into the suffering that he and others experienced because of what is presented to us in our families and communities. He learned early on that we cannot expect to avoid our acquired trauma and cannot expect to be affected by it. He did not bury these thoughts or hang on to his immediate emotional response to things, as many of us do. His search for meaning was very much related to how he should make decisions about his life and the effect of his decisions on the lives of others. He didn't present this way to others, but his inner life and his growing intellectual honesty about things did bring him what I now see was a necessary and productive stress, along with an anxiety that was part of his vision for Mexico. I think his personal action and his political actions showed, implicitly, that he saw that the basic and perhaps ultimate meaning in life was a search for happiness and peace for self and others, including what he called "the evil ones," and that these things are intrinsically linked. This is not a rare belief, but it is a rare conviction that manifests in action. I think that Miguel was able to courageously and with integrity demonstrate this conviction in the bravery he showed in his political actions, which were in conflict even with his own cabinet, many of his friends, and sometimes with me and other family members.

Mexican politicians have not inherited a legacy of credibility, and Miguel was no exception. His conviction that he, as any political leader, must not only head or be a member of a political party but also love, educate, and motivate, was not initially or easily recognized as genuine. The credibility he gained was not related to political action per se, but through his integrity, related to compassion and understanding of the plight of the sector of our population that has become a permanent underclass in Mexico—the poor and marginalized. He became aware of this in a way that not many politicians do. He saw this underclass as a very real problem in terms of the suffering of people, but also as a symptom of what else was wrong in Mexico. He saw this great difference in opportunity as a result of corrupt personal behavior and not primarily because of governmental policies or the structures of administration.

I think he anguished at the mystery of the inconsistencies of the parallels and non-parallels in individual and collective behavior—this great discrepancy and the resulting global problems that now confront the world because of lack of political leadership in a now very small world.

Some of his other writing included exploration of the relationship between personal ethics, and he wrote about clearly seeing that those who acted with a code of ethics and morality were happier. He wanted this for Mexicans. He wanted us to see that at the base of our problems was corrupt individual behavior.

Miguel's formal political legacy was explored for months after his death. His death and the deaths of so many others in the horrible crash that suggested murder and assassination brought a lot of attention, not only within Mexico but in all the world.

Mexico, and indeed all of Latin America, paid little heed to the Miguel's extraordinary attempts to educate and motive or his weekly broadcasts. It seemed that the factor that Miguel spoke about so clearly in his writing—this horrible fatalistic attitude that corruption and greed would not change in Mexico, seemed to prevail, along with the strong conviction that it might well be wasted effort to draw attention to it.

He perhaps will be most remembered by some for being the Empty Piñata President, but chiefly by those who do not see the simplicity of what he was saying, and want to make something more complicated out of it.

In addition to the somewhat fatalistic attitude of Mexicans, I see also another factor that prevented a greater acknowledgment of Miguel's efforts to combat corruption. When we are in an emotionally vulnerable state, we often cling to any seemingly responsible and strong voice that leads us out of our anguish. I think that this occurs individually and collectively. Mexicans and Mexico was in a state of shock and anguish at the time of Miguel's and the others' deaths. Political and religious liturgical actions took place throughout the country; many of the eulogies expressed genuine sorrow, remorse, and praise of Miguel. Those who held the belief that Miguel and the others were murdered also expressed sorrow and praise, along with calls for retaliation and vengeance, but few spoke of Miguel's efforts in relation to his plan or any evaluations of success with this. Cardinal Contreras, as one of these strong voices, was no exception.

The funeral mass held at the cathedral was a great tribute to Miguel. The cardinal spoke of his friendship with Miguel and our families and of his great contribution in being the president and of the great challenges that faced any politician in Mexico. At the background of his words was a kind of attitude that spoke chiefly to the elite of Mexico, to the powerful and rich. He came from the elite, and his authoritarian way of speaking echoed this. Cardinal Contreras did not speak of Miguel's attempts to educate and motivate us to change our personal behavior or about his efforts to deal with the root causes of the corruption in Mexico. He did not honour Miguel by talking of the injustices and poverty. He simply did not understand what Miguel was doing, or perhaps he only saw this as the ethical and moral domain of clerics. His strong voice and the voices of many other governmental officials and social leaders in Mexico repeated similar respectful eulogies, lacking honour for the real value of Miguel's life and work as president.

In addition to the attention given to his presidency and his tragic death, the international community did give a lot of attention to Miguel's plan. Through various media and written tributes that I personally received, I became aware that Miguel and all of his "team" were informally and formally connected and involved in various worldwide organizations that were working to promote the ideas and the values that he was encouraging. Héctor, Isabel, and Miguel often mentioned this connection and movement, but I did not pay much attention to this at the time. I was supported by the many tributes and condolences that came to me, and I became more aware that Miguel's efforts were also linked to formal worldwide movements and to important political and social leaders. This included David Lalonde, the former prime minister of Canada, and others who also talked a little about their efforts in the condolences sent to me.

The weekly broadcasts were stopped shortly after Miguel's death. The new presidency was simply not prepared to continue or to allow those who were now organizing and preparing the presentation to continue under government sponsorship. The discontinuation of the broadcasts seemed a part of not so much the disinterest that many had toward Miguel's plan, but the belief that that particular approach to combating corruption and the resulting unhappiness was simply not accepted as valid. There were and are other priorities.

Miguel's team was determined to continue with the weekly broadcasts and appealed to the new administration to allow them to continue. They were flatly refused, and follow-up attempts, bringing support and recommendations from various sources, were not successful. It was simply out of the question. This did not deter them from forming what today is known as *Las Charlas Miguel*, The Miguel Talks. They broadcast every second week and have amplified the program to include international guest speakers and interviews with Mexicans from various levels of society. At first the cost seemed to prevent them from continuing, but as information about this became known, support came—not only from the media for free air time, but from various educators, groups, churches, and others throughout Mexico, France, the United Kingdom, Canada, Germany, Peru, and the United States of America. They are now able to operate and pay the enormous expenses that are involved. They are now also writing a monthly journal that is prepared and published in conjunction with other international publications.

My initial disappointment with the lack of interest and enthusiasm for a continuation of what Miguel was trying to do eventually subsided, with a greater realization that there was indeed a great interest and support for this in all of Mexico, and indeed in the entire world.

Initially I thought of what Miguel was trying to do in more of an isolated way, not seeing that he was a part of what was happening all over the world and that these things are a part of the teachings that have been presented to us in many ways and in different times. The resistance is our struggle to clearly see and adapt the truths that show us how to live with ourselves and in harmony with others. I see now that Miguel was struggling to tell us in a way that we would understand within the context of Mexico and the suffering we endure because of our ignorance and greed. He knew that insight and wisdom are liberating and that the true nature of the reality of things is what will bring us the freedom to work together to live in relative peace.

I think that Miguel saw the essential role of president as an educator. I see now also that the great opposition to discrediting the belief that tenets, dogmas, or creeds bring transformation is so strong in Mexico and perhaps worldwide, that the struggle to oppose it is a struggle against invested interests of those who hold immense power and often seems like a losing battle. Miguel continued in this struggle and perhaps lost his life because of it.

Miguel's story is not unlike all of ours. It is unique in that in a country gone mad, a world gone mad, he was about to courageously create a way to shed some of the trauma from the past and preplace it with value of service to others. He showed a way to not succumb to the conflict in the world and valiantly exhibit the values that were revealed to him. Many of us are so immersed in the values that are presented to us apart from our inner life that we mistake these for our lives and build walls that prevent our inner growth and inhibit our finding the meaning of life itself. Miguel somehow managed to break away from this, and in doing so, he helped make Mexico and the world a better place. He may well be initially best remembered as the Empty Piñata President, but he was a part of a greater and powerful voice that is indeed changing Mexico and the world. He often cited others as his teachers. Miguel, too, was a great teacher.

"The Miguel Talks," which are now very popular and listened to by many, continually bring an abundance of evidence in the lectures, interviews, and discussion to indicate that Mexico and Mexicans were and are indeed becoming aware that our situation is out of control and are willing to acknowledge that extraordinary efforts are necessary.

Destructive climate change, the pollution of air and water, exploding populations, murderous radical ideologies, depletion of natural resources, poverty, endless wars, ethnic and religious hatred, and greed fed by corruption continue worldwide. In Mexico, the corruption, murders, assaults, rapes, thefts, robberies, burglaries, and frauds continue. Many of these are clearly linked to the production, movement, sale, and consumption of illegal drugs. Corruption in general and corruption in law enforcement and in the judiciary, crimes against journalists and women, and human rights violations are still rampant. Governmental initiatives continue primarily as actions of force. In spite of all this, change, however slowly, is taking place.

The very disagreeable things that loom around us at times, often keep me from sustaining hope, but somehow I come back to this hope in various ways. Just now a sadness and longing for some greater sense of peace and lacking the presence of Miguel bring me only thoughts of going to Santa Rosa, not to escape because of fear or despair, but to reflect, rest, and return with renewed insight, courage, resolve, and optimism. I will be reminded of my need, our need, to be aware, to be present to others with compassion, to act with equanimity and justice, and also to live within ourselves. I will also be reminded that our manifest actions affect others upon whom we are dependant, not as saviours, but as collaborators in our search for peaceful unity and happiness.

Lalo, Malena, Maribel, Nacho, and I have made a plan to meet at Santa Rosa for a weekend visit, a weekend of refuge. I will go with great joy to be with them and to be renewed by the beautiful spirit of innocence, hope, happiness, enthusiasm, and love of my four dear *nietos*. We will enjoy the great gift of Santa Rosa. We will remember Diego, Marta Ana, and Olivia, and we will remember our dear Miguel and how we all continue to benefit in so many ways from his enduring and hopeful gift of compassion, example of endurance, and authenticity.

EPILOGUE

Elusive Hope of Ultimate Right Consequence

We live in a world that is facing so many problems, and many are reaching a crisis state—a state where only extraordinary efforts and interventions might perhaps turn things around and prevent our extinction. The factors involved in the deterioration and the failure of so many aspects of society are extremely complex, but at the heart of possible solutions to these complex issues is individual personal behavior, which leads to or extends to collective efforts that are from consensus, formed by non-partisan and selfless decision-making. Decision-making that stems from the practices of the ancients is now part of our efforts, which bear witness to the fact that we are all one and that we share a common being, movement, and destiny. Our one mind and the seen and unseen efforts of this awareness may even now be working to complement the knowledge of those teachers who have reminded us to believe and apply the things we know, not for ourselves, but for others first. They are telling us or reminding us of the illusion of separateness.

Morality and ethics arise from our interactions, forming contracts of behavior with one another. Although we can identify these and aspire to live by them, we are caught up in smaller and very diverse beliefs, metaphors, fears, and theories that prevent us from agreement on various issues, issues that are threatening our very existence. In our compulsive need to practice our partisan petty beliefs, we sacrifice morals and ethics and refuse to collaborate with one another. Our petty compulsive holding on to emotional issues, sometimes encouraged by a sense of nationalism or regionalism, prevents us from cooperation that would lead to peaceful coexistence and improved quality of life for all people.

We fail to see that the world has no borders and that fighting over these non-existent invisible lines causes great damage and suffering. These non-existent borders are held in place by "non-existent" differences or differences that spring from greed, selfishness, and the need to control. In terms of human wellbeing, these things, in extreme, are nothing short of mental illnesses that are preventing a balance in the functioning of people throughout the world. A paradox exists in that world leaders who simply refuse to, or do not know how to lead, let alone cooperate with one another; hold the control here. When the Christian saviour said that "the poor we will always have with us," or something similar, he was commenting not so much on an economic condition but on the fundamental human nature and the greed, selfishness, and control that we hold over one another.

Whether or not humanity will collectively reach a point where there is a great change in the leadership of people, including the confrontation with one another to conform to standards that promote human life instead of destroying it, remains to be seen. The tyrants that currently control life to the extent of preventing development and allowing great poverty and suffering of those within the invisible borders of their domains, physical and otherwise, are allowed to do so by those whose false values accept the invisible borders and refuse to remove the tyrants. Both are guilty of holding people as hostages and causing them to suffer great poverty, often in great ignorance of their rights and freedoms.

The issues are crucial if survival is expected for the human race. Those who have it within their power to alter the advancing state of decline of society are incapable of acting or refuse to do so. It appears that like individual human lives that end in death, so too will our human world die. Perhaps the death of the world, as certain as our individual deaths, is the natural and inevitable conclusion to our collective being. For those who might hold this to be true, it does not preclude working to improve the quality of collective life in the same way that it does not preclude improving the quality of life for individuals in our search for happiness and peace. This is where we truly find meaning that is somehow akin to a promise of hope for ultimate justice in a life beyond the tangible world we are currently in. Thus, let us continue to begin again and again, as we have done for millennia, performing this action of service to others that holds this—even if somewhat elusive—hope of ultimate right consequence.

The practical application of our dual role in society – living with meaning and practicing our values as well as advocating within the organizational structures where we find meaning with others, will bring about unity and change. The eventual breaking of the piñata by one, is accomplished by the efforts of many in a process that weakens the barriers to its rich treasures that are available to all.

READING GUIDE

1. What was your general experience with this book?

2. What were your expectations? Did the book fulfill them?

3. Did you like the book? Did you enjoy it? Why or why not?

4. Is the title of particular significance to you? Explain.

5. Was the plot of immediate interest to you?

6. How would you describe the book to someone else?

7. Describe the principal characters…their personality, motivations, and other qualities.

8. Describe the relationships between the principal characters.

9. Did their affiliations or past life experiences influence their behavior? How? Why?

10. Do you like the characters? Do they remind you of people you know? Do you approve of their actions—their behavior?

11. Do you have a favorite character?

12. Which character did you relate to most? Why?

13. Do the actions of the principal characters seem plausible? How so?

14. Do you think that this story would make a good movie?

15. Does the behavior of the characters change in the course of the story? Why?

16. Is the plot engaging? Is the story interesting? Is it plausible?

17. Did the complications—the twists and turns in the story surprise you?

18. What themes, ideas, or issues does the author explore? How important are these to you or to others?

19. Does the author use symbols to reinforce the main ideas? Do these or a particular one add to the interest or understanding of the story?

20. How does the particular setting figure in the book?

21. Why do you think that the author chose to tell the story within the particular setting?

22. Is there a specific passage or phrase that you found of particular interest—which 'resonated' with you and your beliefs or thoughts?

23. Is the ending satisfying? If so, why? If not, why not? How would you change it?

24. If you could ask the author a question, what would you ask?

25. Has this novel changed you—broadened your perspective? Have you learned anything new or been exposed to different ideas? Did it create a renewed interest in the theme or the values expressed in the story?

26. How would you summarize this book? What was the intent of the author?

27. Would you recommend this book to other readers? To your friends?

CPSIA information can be obtained
at www.ICGtesting.com
Printed in the USA
BVHW082315180121
597996BV00004B/219